IN THE K
CARPET

"You have been given a royal gift and a task which you must perform. It is your adventure . . . You alone must decide when to use this stone," said the Emperor.

Princess Anah was surprised when her royal birthday gift turned out to be nothing more than a stone on a golden chain. But this ordinary-looking stone could have great power in the Kingdom of the Carpet Dragon. It was up to the Princess to discover what that power was, and when and how to use it . . .

Accompanied by her lovable, loyal and remarkably clumsy pet dragon, Doxa, the Princess sets out on her quest — with some surprising results.

In the
Kingdom of
the Carpet Dragon

Ralph Batten

Illustrations by Toni Goffe

A LION PAPERBACK
Oxford · Batavia · Sydney

Copyright © 1989 Ralph Batten

Published by
Lion Publishing plc
Peter's Way, Sandy Lane West, Littlemore, Oxford
ISBN 0 7459 1533 7
Lion Publishing Corporation
1705 Hubbard Avenue, Batavia, Illinois 60510, USA
ISBN 0 7459 1533 7
Albatross Books Pty Ltd
PO Box 320, Sutherland, NSW 2232, Australia
ISBN 0 7324 0054 6

British Library Cataloguing in Publication Data
Batten, Ralph
In the kingdom of the carpet dragon
I. Title   II. Goffe, Toni
823′.914   [J]

ISBN 0-7459-1533-7

Printed and bound in Great Britain by
Cox and Wyman Ltd, Reading

Contents

There is a legend that tells of a strange and wonderful carpet. It is said that this carpet was made very long ago and that its pattern of hills and lakes and forests shows a land far to the east that could once be found at the place where the sun rises. A land that was called the Kingdom of the Carpet Dragon.

Some even say that this carpet was itself woven there and that is why its colours are so unusual.

For according to this legend, that carpet longs to tell its story. And so it is that if anyone should now find it and look carefully at its faded patterns, with the first light of the newly risen sun shining on it, they might just see the Kingdom of the Carpet Dragon come once more to life . . .

1

The Emperor's Gift

There was a problem in the Kingdom of the Carpet Dragon.

"My Imperial Master!" pleaded the Keeper of the Royal Diary, in his usual serious and solemn way, bowing so low to the Emperor that it looked as if he would do a forward somersault. "It is now only two days until —" He struggled to straighten up. But unfortunately he trod on one of the tassels that hung from the wide green belt that gathered his long, flowing robe together, and so lost something of his usual dignity. "Until," he continued, still bent double and trying to tug the troublesome tassel free, "until the Royal Birthday! And we still haven't decided what to give your Royal Daughter for a present!" He looked up at the Emperor as solemnly as his strange position would allow. For birthdays in the Kingdom of the Carpet Dragon were taken very seriously. In fact, the celebrations for a special birthday could last for several days.

And this was going to be a *very* special birthday.

The Emperor, seated upon a simple wooden cross-legged chair that stood on a beautifully woven carpet, looked at his four assembled advisers and at the Empress who sat beside him. They each in turn looked most worried, as indeed they might. For it is no easy task to choose a birthday present for an Emperor's daughter.

There was a long silence while everyone thought deeply.

The Keeper of the Royal Diary, being a serious sort of person, scratched his head through the beautifully embroidered dome-shaped cap he always wore, and thought very solemn thoughts. For he recalled with a shudder last year's birthday celebrations. How they had given the Emperor's daughter a very large and very sensible silken bonnet.

"Just the thing," he had thought, "for a Royal Princess of the Kingdom." Until he had seen it some days later, looking remarkably like a silken kite complete with dangling string, stuck high up in a huge cedar tree that grew in the middle of the Emperor's garden.

The Collector of the Royal Books, who stood next to the Keeper of the Royal Diary, shook his head slowly, so that his long, wispy, white beard swung gently from side to side. Being a rather sleepy sort of person, he tried to think very peaceful thoughts. But all he could recall, before he finally dozed off again, was how the Emperor's daughter had once been given a set of books called *A Complete History of the Kingdom in Twelve Volumes.*

"Just the thing," he had thought, "for a Royal Princess of the Kingdom." Until he had found eleven of them stacked up in a tower beside the huge cedar tree that grew in the middle of the Emperor's garden, with the Royal Princess balanced on the top, holding the twelfth volume, as she tried to reach what looked like a silken kite that was stuck in the topmost branches of the tree.

The Guardian of the Royal Treasures, who was a very busy sort of person and was always coming or going somewhere, rocked gently to and fro. Fortunately, like everyone else in the Kingdom he wore curly-toed carpet slippers, which may not have been very practical for coming or going, but certainly made rocking to and fro considerably easier. Rocking helped him think – and he was trying hard to think very helpful thoughts. But all he could remember was how the Emperor's daughter had once been given a beautiful golden tiara.

"Just the thing," he had thought, "for a Royal Princess of the Kingdom." Until he had seen pineapples being catapulted from the Princess's bedroom. Apparently she had tied a piece of elastic to each end of the tiara and attached the other ends to two poles of her four-poster bed. She had thereby created a pineapple-shooting catapult. She was, it turned out later, aiming at a silken kite stuck high up in a cedar tree that grew in the middle of the Emperor's garden.

The Royal Carpenter, who stood slightly apart from the other three Royal Advisers, had given up thinking altogether. He stuck his huge hands deep into the pockets of the leather apron that he wore over his coarse, woven robe and loose-fitting trousers and, being a practical sort of person, wondered what the Emperor's daughter was doing at that moment.

Well, at that precise and particular moment, the Royal Princess of the Kingdom of the Carpet Dragon was halfway up the rough stone wall that surrounded the Emperor's island. She wanted to think, and she knew that the very best thinking place in the whole Kingdom was on top of this wall. From there she could view the one and only gateway that led into the Emperor's city, and at low tide she could also see the sixty-six stepping stones that reached out across the lake to the woodlands beyond. From this wall she would watch people as they came and went. Some stepped cautiously from stone to stone, concentrating on each movement. Others confidently strode across the lake, apparently taking little notice of where they would place their foot next. The Princess was very proud of the fact that she could cross all sixty-six stepping stones, walking backwards with her eyes closed.

The Princess, who only rarely wore the delicate and beautifully embroidered flowing robes of the Kingdom such as the Empress wore and who much preferred to be called "Anah" rather than her proper name (which was Shanahtina), was dressed in a simple woven tunic. Even in yellow curly-toed slippers she had soon scrambled to the top of the wall. Below, watching her climb, sat a dragon.

Now, in the Kingdom, dragons are very rare. But they aren't at all frightening. Well, not normally. And they aren't particularly big. This one was bright purple and instead of having scales, as some dragons are supposed to have, he was covered with what appeared to be tufts of wool. More like a shaggy carpet. And, indeed, that was the reason why such dragons were known as Carpet Dragons. As far as anyone knew they were only to be found in the Emperor's Kingdom, which was just as well, for the people who lived in the land were extremely good at weaving carpets. And they seemed to have a special liking for such dragons, even if they did have something of a reputation for always being near at hand when trouble occurred. Nonetheless, the people were happy for their land to be known as the Kingdom of the Carpet Dragon.

Now this particular Carpet Dragon had wings which were bright yellow, and looked more like canvas than leather. He had a long tail with a flat point at the end, which he didn't ever seem to have under complete control. He had certainly never tried to breathe fire, for he had always felt that would be an incredibly silly thing for a Carpet Dragon to do. And he doubted if it would work, anyway. In fact Doxa – for that was his name – doubted just about *everything*.

Right now he was doubting that his Princess would ever reach the top of the wall. But when she did, and then turned, looked down and called, "Come on, you can come up as well. It's easy!" he doubted that he had any choice in the matter. Doxa disliked heights. It was partly for that reason that he had never tried to fly. He also doubted, of course, that his wings would actually work. And, if they did, he doubted they would continue working once they had got him off the ground. So he decided that it was far safer not to try. Doxa preferred to walk. Indeed, he was particularly pleased with the bright red curly-toed carpet slippers that he wore on his feet.

By now Doxa was halfway up the wall. He had got to that point where he doubted whether he would reach the top but, even more worrying, he wasn't sure that he could reach the ground either.

"Oh come on! Here, let me help," insisted Anah, reaching down and grabbing one of Doxa's front claws. She had been tempted to grab his tail, which was draped over his left shoulder, but she knew it was a very unwise thing to pull a dragon's tail. Even a Carpet Dragon's. Anyway, with considerable scrabbling of feet, flapping of wings, closing of eyes and bruising of nose, Doxa, the Carpet Dragon, was eventually sitting on top of the wall next to his Princess.

"Well, Doxa, in two days' time it's my Royal Birthday!" She paused to let the full significance of that fact sink into the dragon's head.

For when a child of the Emperor reached the age to have her Royal Birthday, she had to learn to be a Real Princess. Now there was more to being a Royal Princess than most people realize. She would, of course, have to change her name. No longer would she be simply called Anah. No, from then on she would have to be called "The Royal Princess Shanahtina". And she was sure she would also have to learn to cope with golden tiaras, and of course how to curtsey, and how to walk solemnly and sensibly. She would also have to learn about the Kingdom. No doubt there would be long lists of dates and names and facts and figures to memorize. In short, she would have to learn to do all the things she disliked most.

Anah was not at all sure that she wanted to learn to be a Real Princess. And so it was with a little misgiving that she looked forward to her Royal Birthday. Then suddenly – as if a much better thought had occurred to her – she turned to the dragon, her eyes bright with excitement.

"Doxa, what do you think they'll give me for my Royal Birthday present?"

Doxa doubted that she would get anything, after the slight problems of last year.

But he hoped she would, for he knew that she was not at all ungrateful for the presents she had been given. She had enjoyed them very much and had said so to everyone. It was just that sometimes she saw things a little differently from other people and used things in a slightly unusual way. He was very proud of his Princess.

"I hope they won't give me a silken bonnet again, or *The Complete History of the Kingdom in Twelve Volumes*, and I really don't need another golden tiara. Oh . . . I hope . . . I wish that I'll be given something very special this year." And she looked hopefully at Doxa the Carpet Dragon.

In fact the Princess's Royal Birthday gift was still causing considerable problems to the Emperor's advisers.

The Royal Carpenter, being a man of few words, sighed deeply.

"Mmm," he said in a deep, rough way that sounded like a saw splintering through wood. In fact, he was a man of so few words that most people had never actually heard him say anything other than "Mmm". He could, of course, on occasions say much more. But normally he chose to say only "Mmm". Fortunately he could say it in many different ways. This way seemed to mean that he couldn't think of anything at all and, to be honest, neither could the other Royal Advisers.

"My Royal Master," pleaded the Keeper of the Royal Diary again, still as solemnly, but bowing less low and more carefully. "As this is the Princess's Royal Birthday, for a change, couldn't *you* suggest something that we could give her for a present?"

Now, as the Keeper of the Royal Diary said this, the Emperor's dark eyes seemed to twinkle strangely.

Unlike his advisers, he did not wear the brightly-coloured, loose-fitting robes that most people wore in the Kingdom. Indeed, it was not his clothes that made him so noble, not even his cloak of pure woven gold, nor the fact that he ruled over many lands. No, it was simply that without a doubt he was an Emperor of royal descent. Some said he was a descendant of the Great Weaver himself. He was tall and strong, but gentle and wise. His skin was dark, and his hair and beard looked as if the wild east wind had combed them.

"Yes," continued the Emperor rather mysteriously. "Perhaps for a change I *can* suggest something. But, Carpenter, may I first borrow from you a small hammer?"

The Carpenter agreed, with a positive but quizzical "Mmm", and then the bewildered and astonished advisers were sent away with the Emperor's thanks that they had been such a great help, and a promise that they would all have a part to play in giving the Princess her Royal Birthday present.

By the following day the Emperor's gift was ready, and by the morning of the first day of Anah's Royal Birthday everything had been prepared. A grand party had been arranged. All had been invited. Even the Princess's dragon.

Now Doxa had never really got the hang of table manners, and although the Princess had repeatedly explained to him that it was rather rude to sit with your tail lying on the table, she didn't seem to understand that his tail simply could not be trusted. If the truth were known, Doxa felt very sorry for the Keeper of the Royal Diary who happened to be sitting next to him. It was simply most unfortunate that his tail had suddenly decided to flip up on to the table at the exact moment that the Keeper of the Royal Diary had reached out for a particularly squishy piece of jam cake. Doxa's tail came down smartly on the poor man's hand, which duly flattened the piece of cake. The jam spurted out and would have perhaps caused terrible damage to the carefully-woven wall-hangings that decorated the room, had not the Guardian of the Royal Treasures chosen that precise moment to stand up. Now, because he was rather short, the low-flying jam caught him just below the nose and then proceeded to drip off his drooping moustache. There was a moment of utter silence. Doxa removed his tail and replaced it on the floor behind him. He doubted that anyone could possibly understand how terribly difficult life could be for a dragon. The Princess stuffed a handkerchief in her mouth to try to stifle her laugh, until her face had turned as red as Doxa's eyes.

The Emperor, being very wise, decided that perhaps the time had come to give the Princess her gift. He stood up as the Guardian of the Royal Treasures sat down to squeeze the remaining jam from his moustache, muttering, "Oh, drat that dragon's tail."

"My child," the Emperor began, bringing order once more to the room. "This is your Royal Birthday gift." He gave the Princess a small package. She could easily hold it in one hand. Obviously it was not *The Complete History of the Kingdom in Twelve Volumes*. Nor was it another golden tiara. And Doxa doubted whether even the Great Emperor could get a sensible silken bonnet into such a small parcel.

The Princess opened the package and carefully took out a small, rough stone that hung from a beautifully-crafted golden chain.

"Thank you," replied the Princess, unsure of what she really felt.

"My child," repeated the Emperor, taking her gently by the hand and gazing deeply into her dark eyes. "This is no ordinary gift. This stone can have great power. For although this stone can never change itself, it can be used to change one thing in this Kingdom – but one thing only. It is your task to use this stone wisely."

Anah's eyes opened wide in total astonishment. So did those of the Royal Advisers. There was a buzz of excitement from around the room.

"Remember, Anah," echoed the Empress gently. "It can only change one thing. And, Anah, there are two more things you must know about this stone. First, it must be used before the end of your Royal Birthday celebration. And second, it will only work if this Palace is kept in sight, for it must be used in this Kingdom."

Anah gazed almost in disbelief at the wonderful gift she had in her hands. And then suddenly she thought of all the things she would like to change. All those things she disliked most.

The boring lessons.

The cold, wet days.

The horrible-tasting, mushy vegetables that were supposed to be good for her.

The heavy, irritating, uncomfortable golden tiaras.

In her mind the list just seemed to go on and on. Which one would she choose? Even after just a few moments' thought she realized that it might be quite difficult to make a decision.

"But what shall I change?" she whispered, more to herself than to anyone else. The stone had begun to feel slightly heavier in her hand as she thought of the responsibility of the gift.

"*That* will be your adventure," replied the Emperor gently. Anah gazed deeply into her father's dark eyes and began to wonder just why she had been given this gift. For there was something rather mysterious in her father's look. Perhaps there was something that she alone (with the help of the stone, of course) could change. Perhaps her father wanted her to do a special task with the power of this stone. But what could it be? Perhaps her father had entrusted her with a task more important than simply to change the taste of squishy, slimy, boiled swede!

"But," continued the Emperor, "we shall all help you. And so will the Great Weaver."

Anah looked quizzically at her father. Oh, she had, of course, heard of the Great Weaver before. Everyone that lived in the Kingdom of the Carpet Dragon knew that the Great Weaver had made their world and everything in it. Indeed, she knew he had made all worlds. But the Great Weaver had always seemed distant and far away to Anah. She had never seen him, and wasn't sure that anyone had. But strangely, whenever he was mentioned, she always felt rather warm inside.

She could, of course, have asked one of the Royal Tutors to tell her more about the Great Weaver, but they made everything seem so dull and boring; and she didn't want the Great Weaver to be like that. So she had never asked. Could the Great Weaver really help her? She looked at the assembled advisers, who all looked a little uncomfortable. Particularly the Guardian of the Royal Treasures who was still having trouble with a sticky moustache, and sat glaring at the Carpet Dragon's tail.

Doxa, however, hardly noticed. For he did not like what he had heard about adventures. And he had a strange feeling that if his Princess was to set out on an adventure to use this stone, then it would almost certainly involve him. Doxa doubted he would like adventures. He had once met one in a dream and had not enjoyed the experience. He doubted that a real-life adventure would be any more pleasant.

By now it was beginning to grow dark. So the Empress took a wax taper and lit it from one of the birthday candles that burned dimly on the banqueting table. With this taper she lit an oil lamp that hung from the wall.

The Princess of the Kingdom of the Carpet Dragon was beginning to be intrigued by the turn her Royal Birthday had taken. She opened her hand and looked down at the golden chain and the small rough stone, and then returned to her seat. As she did so she bent her head and whispered into Doxa's ear, "This Royal Birthday might be better than we thought!"

Doxa doubted that the Princess had any idea what he was thinking, even though she was the Princess in the Kingdom of the Carpet Dragon.

2

The Song-Box

The Princess of the Kingdom of the Carpet Dragon longed to get started on her adventure. She was eager to find out what it was in the Kingdom that she could change, although she had no idea how she would use the stone, nor how this stone would work. She only knew that if the Emperor had given it to her there could be no doubt that the stone would indeed work.

The Emperor looked kindly at her. "My child, it is now the end of the first day of your Royal Birthday celebrations and you have been given a Royal Gift, and a task which you must perform. It is your adventure – and yours alone. For you alone must decide when to use this stone."

Doxa suddenly felt a glimmer of hope. Perhaps, after all, this adventure wouldn't involve him. His tail flicked up on to his left shoulder — which it normally did when he was fairly pleased about something. The Emperor noticed the movement and continued in a slightly louder and more solemn voice.

"However, others can be of some help." The Princess turned to her Carpet Dragon and smiled excitedly and nodded enthusiastically. Doxa's tail slid from his shoulders and thumped onto the ground behind him.

"For the Royal Advisers will also give you a gift. As you know, at a Royal Birthday an Emperor's child must learn about the Kingdom he or she will one day rule over. And they must also learn about the Great Weaver who made it."

At this point Anah fully expected one of the two Royal Tutors to be called in to begin to teach her about the Kingdom and how to be a Real Princess. They were kind, but incredibly boring. They wore long, dark tunics and they always seemed to carry equally long and uninteresting scrolls of yellowed paper bearing endless lists of dates and names and tedious rules.

But the Royal Tutors did not appear. Instead the Emperor continued, "Each of the Royal Advisers will, in turn, tell you a story. A story that will teach you about this Kingdom and the Great Weaver who made it. Listen carefully, for there is much wisdom in these stories and, who knows, they may help you decide how you must use your gift.

"Tonight the Carpenter will tell you his story. It is his gift to you. For tonight you shall learn where the woods and forests that surround our Kingdom came from."

Anah turned to look at the huge and slightly awkward figure of the Royal Carpenter.

The Carpenter in turn looked down gently at the dejected Carpet Dragon.

"Mmm . . ." he began. His rasping voice cut through the slightly smoky atmosphere. Doxa hoped that his tail would behave itself — but doubted that it would. Then the Carpenter looked at the Princess.

"Princess," he gently growled. "The Great Weaver has made many worlds."

The Carpenter lifted his huge hands as if to show just how many. "Each of them has its own pattern and weaves its own story." And with that the Carpenter gave the Princess the gift of his story. Although, since he was a man of such few words, the Princess was never quite sure afterwards if it was the Carpenter's voice or the Carpenter's hands that told the tale. Whichever it was, the Princess never forgot it.

For it was about a cat. A cat with pure, white fur and cunning green eyes. Now this cat happened to live in a land of forests and woods where the noblest of all work was that of a carpenter. Indeed, in that land, the Great Weaver was called the Carpenter.

The boastful cat wished all animals to think her the most important creature in all of that land. And so, of course, she lived in a carpenter's workshop. But the carpenter she chose to live with was very poor and couldn't afford to make things from new wood. So instead he took what was old or broken or useless and made beautiful things from them.

One day the poor carpenter found a small wooden box that had once been used by a noble lady to hold a gift for her husband. Now this gift was a delicious and rare fruit, and once the gift had been unwrapped, the wooden box had been thrown away.

The carpenter had found the old box and taken it back to his shop. And then, one evening, as he sat at his workbench, his eyes suddenly twinkled, and a broad smile spread across his kindly face. For he had decided what was to be made from the old box.

"This shall be a song-box." And with that he went happily to bed.

Now the boastful cat had overheard all that the carpenter had said and decided that she could make the song-box without the help of the carpenter. Then she saw a rabbit hop and jump past the wooden workshop door. "Hey, Rabbit," she called out, "come and see my song-box!"

Of course this rabbit had never seen a song-box before and although he was a little suspicious of the cat he was also rather curious. And so he turned aside and went in to the workshop to see the song-box.

"Well," purred the cat proudly, licking her front paws as she did so. "Do you know anyone else that has a song-box in their home?"

The rabbit shook his head until his ears flopped so quickly from side to side that they became quite knotted. Clearly he was most impressed.

But it so happened that a small mouse who, much to the annoyance of the cat, also lived in the carpenter's shop, had likewise overheard the talk about the song-box. And, although he was more than a little afraid of that white cat, he crept out from his hole under the workbench.

"It looks very fine," he squeaked most politely, "but, if you don't mind me mentioning the fact, isn't it rather quiet for a song-box?"

The cat most definitely did mind, and

was tempted to chase this miserable mouse back where it had come from. But now that the question had been asked, the cat knew it would need to be answered.

"Well," spat the cat in a most contemptuous way. "It needs to be played before it will make a song."

"And how, O most wise and clever cat, do you do that?" squeaked the mouse, scurrying up the workbench leg and on to the song-box itself.

Now the cat was greatly tempted to put an end to the irritating mouse's questions once and for all. But the mouse saw the cat's paw move and leaped off the song-box, which toppled over and fell on the floor. As it did so the song-box made a hollow-sounding "clunk".

"Ah!" gasped the rabbit in wonder, unknotting his ears. "The box has sung! Did you hear it, O most wise and noble cat?"

"Of course!" purred the boastful cat, trying to hide her surprise. "Didn't I tell you it was a song-box?"

"O, most clever cat, play it again, please," pleaded the rabbit, folding his long ears back along his neck.

The cat patted at the wooden box with her paw and, sure enough, as the box toppled and rolled there was another hollow clunk.

"It really is a marvel," said the rabbit, "and you, O most noble cat, play it so well."

Now the cat enjoyed flattery and so proceeded to play the song-box for some considerable time. Although the rabbit was most impressed, the little grey mouse eventually made himself heard above the repeated clunks.

"I'm sure the cat does play that tune well, but, if you don't mind me mentioning the fact, isn't that song rather short? Perhaps, O most musical cat, you could play another? Surely it can play more than one note?"

"It can!" spat the cat at the grey mouse, who had made sure that he was near to a convenient hole in the wall. "But," continued the cat purring gently, "I'm tired and need a rest."

"Then can I play it?" interrupted the rabbit. "For, O most exhausted cat, I feel rested after such excellent music."

The cat narrowed her green eyes to a slit and glared at the mouse.

"Very well," purred the cat after a short pause, "but you must carry it on your back and hold it in place with your ears." The rabbit readily agreed, and so the cat and the mouse pushed and pulled the box and eventually got it on the rabbit's back. "Now remember, you must hold it in place with your ears," reaffirmed the cunning cat.

The rabbit grasped the box tightly with his ears and began to leap around the room as energetically as he could. The clunks and bangs that came from the box nearly deafened the poor creature, so that he couldn't really be sure what he was hearing. But, when he eventually collapsed in an exhausted heap, and the cat purred, "That was wonderful, rabbit. Such a beautiful song and so skilfully played," the rabbit felt he could only agree.

The mouse, however, was not so sure. "Yes," he squeaked, "and so very loud. But I wonder, O most patient and kind cat, could it play a sweet song?"

The cat, who was becoming more than a little irritated with this meddling mouse, purred gently and began slowly to wash her whiskers. "Of course," she said after a pause. "But sadly for sweet music it would have to be covered in sweet things."

"Oh, come on then," sighed the exhausted rabbit. "Let's decorate the outside and then it will play a sweet song. Just as our kind cat has said."

And so, as the boastful cat watched with glaring green eyes, the mouse and the rabbit found all sorts of sweet things to cover the song-box with. They put honey and berries and sweet-smelling flowers and sticky buds all over the wooden box until it was quite covered. Then they insisted that the cat be the first to play the sweet music. The cat very gently rolled the box over and, sure enough, instead of a clunk there was a very gentle muffled "thump" from the box.

"See," answered the sly cat, "how sweet and gentle the song is now."

"Oh yes," agreed the spellbound rabbit. "Now, O most tuneful cat, the song is truly different. It is most wonderful music."

"Well," squeaked the mouse once more. "If you don't mind me mentioning the fact, all I can hear is a quiet clunk, which I suppose is a bit better than a loud one."

Now the cat's patience had eventually been exhausted. She hissed and spat at the grey mouse, and suddenly shot out her claws and turned to pounce. But as she did so she spun the song-box across the floor and it smashed into the carpenter's bench. The flowers and buds and berries flew off it and the lid of the box shattered. Then from inside there clunked and thumped and rolled an old, dry fruit stone. For when the nobleman had cut open the delicious fruit that his wife had given him, he had dropped its stone back into the wooden box. The rabbit looked at the splintered song-box, and the old, dry fruit stone.

"Why, O most ridiculous and boastful cat," he sneered, hopping over to the shattered song-box and shaking his head until his ears re-tied on top of his head. "It's only an old box with a dry fruit stone in it. What a foolish and big-headed cat you are. It's not a song-box at all!" And with that he indignantly hopped out of the door.

The mouse said nothing, for he was safely hidden in his nest.

The cat hissed at the broken box which was lit up by the first rays of the morning sun. "What a useless song-box you are!"

Now the carpenter had been woken up by the strange noises in his workshop and, being truly wise, even if he was poor, guessed what had happened when he saw the old battered box on the floor and the dejected white cat sitting under the workbench licking honey from her paws. He went over and picked up the broken and lidless box. He then took some soft wood shavings from the workbench and gently and carefully laid them inside. He took a hammer and nails and went outside the little workshop. The cat watched in bewilderment as the carpenter nailed the box up just above the window, and then returned inside the poor workshop.

"There we are!" he said happily to himself without a hint of boastfulness, but looking at the cat. "A song-box."

The cat could hear nothing. She turned her head from side to side and pricked up her ears. But still nothing could be heard. She crept from beneath the bench and looked up at the window. As she did so, the cat saw two small, bright yellow birds come twittering and flapping past. One flew down into the wooden box and moments later popped back up and flew around the other bird. Then both the small yellow birds darted into the box and there they began to sing a most beautiful song.

The old carpenter smiled gently and said again, "A song-box!"

The boastful cat looked sadly up at the old man and purred gently, for now she knew how very foolish she had been.

There was a long silence in the banqueting hall. Anah wondered if the story was over, when the Emperor softly interrupted, "But that is not quite the end of the story."

Anah looked quizzically at her father.

"For as that carpenter reached down and gently stroked the purring cat he found the fruit stone lying on the floor. The carpenter picked it up. And, Princess, it was a very good thing that he did so. For some say that the poor carpenter was none other than the Great Weaver himself, the maker of all worlds. Others say that the fruit stone he took was planted in our land and there it grew into a tree, and from that tree grew the huge forests that surround this lake and this city. And whenever we look at those mighty trees put there by the Great Weaver, and we listen to the birds that sing in their branches, we remember that proud cat and the song-box, and how foolish it would be for even an Emperor of the Kingdom to boast about what he thinks he can do without the help of the Great Weaver.''

But Anah was hardly listening, for she was too busy looking at the stone and thinking again of what she would change in the Kingdom of the Carpet Dragon.

3

The Log-Lift

The Princess of the Kingdom of the Carpet Dragon woke very early the next morning and, as the bright morning sun streamed through the arched windows of her bedroom, she remembered the Emperor's birthday gift. She looked at the small, rough stone that still hung around her neck and muttered, "I wonder if I should use the stone today?"

For she remembered what her mother, the Empress, had said: that the stone must be used before the end of the Royal Birthday celebrations. Perhaps the power in the stone slowly died away — just as a fire slowly burns out. Perhaps every moment it was losing some of its power. If she were to change something really important, perhaps she should use it straight away.

Doxa, who was asleep as usual in the doorway to the Princess's room, was dreaming that he was a true, flying dragon. He was just swooping down to terrorize some vicious pirates, when his troublesome tail fell from the woven cushion he always slept on with such a sharp smack that he woke up with a start. He fully expected to see the room full of cutlass-swinging, scar-faced men. But, instead, he saw the Princess sitting on her bed looking at the strange stone.

"Well, Doxa," Anah announced triumphantly without even looking at the Carpet Dragon. "It's time to go and find something in the Kingdom that needs changing."

Now the problem with having the power to change anything, as Anah was about to find out, is that you never can find something to change. Indeed, even in the Royal Princess's experience, you find things you want to change when you're least able to change them.

It really was most annoying, as Anah was desperate to use the Emperor's gift. She decided that perhaps she should ask the Emperor himself what it was that she should change. But when she went through the royal banqueting room she found her father very busy, trying to organize things for the second day's birthday celebrations. The Guardian of the Royal Treasures was just hurrying off to collect this and that, and the Keeper of the Royal Diary was solemnly warning all who would listen that they would never get everything ready in time and that they really should have started all these preparations yesterday.

Anah decided that now would not be a good time to disturb the Emperor and so she quietly slipped out of the room.

Doxa followed, but sadly his tail couldn't quite resist a quick flip as they passed the Guardian of the Royal Treasures returning to the banqueting room with a large tray of silver knives and forks. The poor man saw the dragon's tail coming and stopped dead in his tracks, which is a most difficult thing to do in curly-toed carpet slippers. He did manage to prevent the dragon's tail from flipping straight on to the tray, but sadly, although he stopped, the knives and forks on the tray did not. They clattered and crashed on to the stone floor.

"Oh drat that dragon's tail!" he muttered, bending down to pick up the fallen objects. But Doxa and the Princess scarcely heard, for they were off searching for something that needed to be changed.

Anah decided that perhaps the Empress would be able to help. But when she found her mother in the Royal Library, busy looking for a book about bonnet-making, Anah decided to slip out again, unnoticed.

She would probably have managed it, had not Doxa's tail chosen that moment to do a sideways flip. Unfortunately the Collector of the Royal Books was standing on a stool reaching up to a high shelf. The dragon's tail knocked the stool clean away from under him, which left the Collector of the Royal Books hanging on to the topmost shelf, his curly-toed carpet slippers not quite reaching the floor.

Doxa and the Princess hurried out of the room as quickly as possible, with Doxa feeling most embarrassed and doubting if his tail would ever learn to behave itself. Meanwhile the Collector of the Royal Books was helped down from the shelf by the Royal Empress herself. He then decided that he had done quite enough for one day and went to sit at his desk in the Royal Library for a quiet snooze.

Anah was becoming desperate to find out how she should use the stone. There was lots she could change, of course. There was, for instance, her room. She didn't really like the incredible mess that it normally got itself into. It was very annoying not to be able to find things amongst the piles of objects and clothes that cluttered the room. She was quite tempted to use the stone to change her room into something that was neat and tidy. It would certainly please her parents. But then she thought that she *could* tidy it herself and

save the stone for something more important. So she didn't use it. She didn't tidy her room either — she was far too busy. After all, time might be running out.

Having searched the whole of the Palace without success, Anah decided to return to her room with Doxa. However, on the way she went past the Royal Music Room and there on a shelf she noticed a shell flute. It was a huge, brightly-coloured, curled sea shell that had come from the Great Ocean, at the mouth of the river that flowed from the lake that surrounded the Emperor's island. It had been beautifully engraved and small holes had been delicately bored into its twisted cone shape. The pointed end of the shell had been cut so as to form a mouthpiece. When you blew down this, the shell made the most curious noise. Anah stepped into the room and, quickly checking that no one was about, she picked up the strange instrument and gently blew it. A soft, sea-like sound filled the room and, as she played, it suddenly seemed as if the room were full of sweet-singing sea birds. Then she remembered the Carpenter's story of the night before.

"Of course!" she thought. "He's so wise. He'll know what it is that I should change." And without even bothering to put down the precious shell flute she shot out of the room, followed by a rather exhausted Carpet Dragon.

She couldn't find the Carpenter in his workshop in the Palace and so she searched throughout the Emperor's city for him. She looked into many of the wooden houses where people sat at the clattering weaving looms, making the beautiful, brightly-coloured carpets for which the Kingdom was so famous.

But the Carpenter was nowhere to be found.

Finally she scrambled up the wall that surrounded the island and there, across the lake, she saw the huge figure of the Royal Carpenter cutting wood with an axe. He was chopping up large trunks into smaller logs and piling them up on the bank.

Anah, followed by Doxa, hurried to the city gate and then down the ramp and out over the sixty-six stepping stones. Doxa was exhausted with all this running and stayed at the city gates. He doubted that his tail could really be trusted anyway and a careless flip or flick while crossing the stones could be most unpleasant. The Princess, however, ran confidently across the sixty-six stones. Doxa was very impressed with his Princess. She reached the Carpenter and breathlessly asked if he could tell her how she could use the stone, before all the power in it had drained away. The Carpenter looked at her.

"Mmm," he sighed, lifting up another huge log. "Why ask me? I am not the Great Weaver." And with that he set off to the lakeside. But then, he always was a man of few words.

Anah, who was used to the Carpenter's ways, was not in any way offended by this brief conversation. Indeed, as far as discussions with the Carpenter went, that had been one of the longer ones she had known. She watched as the Carpenter put his axe into the belt that was tied around his leather apron. She had fully expected him to carry the logs one by one across the stepping stones. But instead he took a thin rope from his leather apron and tied all the logs into a line. He then rolled the chain of logs down to the water and, holding on to one end of the rope, he began to step across the stones, towing all the logs at once across the lake to the Emperor's city. He looked up at the Princess who was watching him with astonishment, and he almost seemed to guess what she was thinking.

"The Great Weaver gave us this lake to use. It is stronger than I am." With that he seemed effortlessly to move the whole tree that he had hewn. Anah watched him step

44

easily from stone to stone towards the city, while overhead some bright yellow birds twittered and sang. Then she decided that there was no point in waiting, and began to cross the stones herself.

Anah noticed Doxa watching the Royal Carpenter move the logs across the lake. It was obvious that the dragon was impressed. Anah was very disappointed that she had not yet used the stone and she also felt rather jealous of the Carpenter's cleverness.

"I'll show that dragon!" thought Anah. "Hey Doxa," she boasted. "That's nothing! Watch me."

Anah promptly closed her eyes, turned around on the third stepping stone and began to hop backwards. She did remarkably well considering she was still carrying the shell. But by the thirtieth stone she was beginning to feel very uneasy. She wished she had not boasted that she could cross the stones in such a ridiculous way. But it was too late to stop. Surprisingly, she managed to reach the sixty-third stepping stone before she slipped. Without thinking, she put out her arms to steady herself and, as she did so, she let go of the precious shell flute. There was a loud plop and a splash as it dropped into the lake and quickly sank to the bottom. The Princess watched in total horror as the ripples spread out over the clear surface of the water.

Doxa, who had observed the entire incident, doubted if he had ever seen anything sink more quickly.

The Princess knelt down on the sixty-third stepping stone. Through the shimmering water she could just see the shell flute lying in the mud at the bottom of the lake. She plunged her arm deep into the cold water, soaking her woven tunic past the elbow, but she just couldn't reach the brightly-coloured shell. The water this close to the island was not that deep, but Anah knew she could never reach it. Suddenly she remembered the Emperor's gift. Maybe this was why she had been given the stone. She would certainly like to change things. She would like to change where the shell flute was. But then she would also like to change the fact that Doxa had watched her slip. Maybe if she used the stone to change the one then the other would happen by itself. But maybe it wouldn't!

"Oh . . ." she mumbled, ". . . if only the stone would work twice . . ." But she remembered what her father had said: the stone itself could not change. And the Empress had been very insistent that it could change only one thing. Besides, she was really quite sure

46

that she had not been given the stone just to get her shell flute back! No . . . she would have to try something else first.

She could have asked for help, but the Princess of the Kingdom of the Carpet Dragon was very independent. Indeed, she was a little worried that if she asked someone to help her, they might start asking awkward questions. Why had she been carrying the shell flute in the first place? Even worse, they might laugh at her for slipping on one of the stepping stones and dropping the shell. She was, after all, very proud of the fact that she could walk across all sixty-six stepping stones backwards with her eyes closed. Anyway, she decided this was no time to ask for help.

Then suddenly she noticed that the Carpenter had piled the logs up at the gateway to the city, and next to the pile of logs he had left the rope which he had used to tow them. She quickly ran up the ramp, collected the rope and a long thin twig from the wood pile, and then she stepped back across the last three stepping stones on to the sixty-third stone.

Doxa watched from a safe distance as Anah made a small loop in the end of the rope. Then she put the knotted end on to the end of the stick and pushed it under the water.

Very carefully she twisted and pushed the twig until the loop in the rope slipped over the pointed end of the cone-shaped shell flute. She then pulled the rope and the loop tightened around the shell. She gently removed the twig and then began to pull the rope harder and harder, but the shell was stuck firmly into the mud at the bottom of the lake. And because the shell was shaped like a curled cone, and because Anah had to pull it slightly from the side, the rope suddenly slipped off the pointed end of the shell.

The Princess very nearly toppled into the lake. She was glad that she didn't, for although she didn't mind getting wet and the water wasn't deep at this point, the bottom of the lake was thick in mud and she knew how very dangerous the mud at the bottom of a lake could be.

Using the rope, Anah knelt down and tried again and again to pull the shell up from the bottom of the lake. But every time she really began to pull, the rope simply slid off the cone-shaped shell. But then finally the rope held tight. Anah pulled and heaved, but simply couldn't budge the shell. Indeed, it seemed that the more she pulled the rope, the deeper the shell settled into the mud, so that soon she could hardly see the shell at all. To add to her misery, her knees were getting very wet.

Then suddenly, to her horror, she realized why. For the sixty-third stepping stone was getting smaller. Well, it looked it. She thought for a moment that the stepping stone was sinking, but then she realized that the same was happening to all the stepping stones. The tide was coming in! The shell was now even deeper under water and mud. Soon she would have to give up altogether because the stepping stones would be completely covered by water.

"Oh Doxa," she cried in desperation to the purple Carpet Dragon watching anxiously from the gateway. "The water in the lake is getting deeper. Oh . . . I shall have to use the stone." Still holding onto the rope with one hand, she reached for the golden chain around her neck with the other. But how could she be sure that this was the thing she had to change? Surely she had only just caused this particular problem — what if she were to waste the Emperor's gift? If only she could be sure. If only someone could help her.

Anah looked about in desperation — and saw the huge figure of the Royal Carpenter standing by the woodpile. Doxa stood next to him, and both of them were watching her. She stood up still holding the rope and for a moment was going to pretend that nothing was wrong. But suddenly that seemed rather silly. For Doxa already knew — not that he could say anything. And strangely she felt the Royal Carpenter knew as well.

She called back across the stones to the ramp.

"I've seen a shell I want to get," she began, avoiding looking into the Carpenter's eyes. "But it's stuck in the mud at the bottom of the lake. Could you get it for me?"

The Carpenter just continued to look at her.

"Please . . . could you get it for me?" tried Anah again.

There was still no response from the Carpenter. Maybe he had seen what had happened. Maybe he had seen her boasting and showing off. Well, if he wasn't going to help her, she would use the stone after all — and then it would be all *his* fault that it hadn't been used properly! She reached again for the stone around her neck — and stopped. She knew she really couldn't use it for such a thing. She must say what had really happened.

"Please Carpenter . . ." she called, "I was showing off while I was carrying the shell flute — and I slipped and dropped it. I shall be in terrible trouble if I don't get it back.

Please will you help me?" Anah looked into the Carpenter's eyes.

"Child," he said in his normal rasping voice. "I cannot get the shell back. Even I don't have that strength." Anah stared at him in disbelief. He was the strongest person in the Kingdom. Surely he could do it? But from the look in his eyes she knew that he was telling the truth. It wasn't that he didn't want to help her — he couldn't help her! She looked down at the rope in her hand, and followed it down through the water to the mud below. There was now no sign of the shell, apart from the occasional bubble that drifted up from the mud. She realized that no one standing on the stepping stones could pull the shell out.

"Child, it would not be good for me to boast about what I cannot do." Anah stared at the woodpile — and suddenly she remembered the Carpenter's story from the night before. She felt as foolish as the boastful cat, but she remembered something else as well.

"The Great Weaver," she cried. "The Great Weaver . . . he got the song-box to work . . . he's powerful and clever, isn't he? He put the trees and the lake here. He can do great things. Maybe he can help us get the shell back!"

The Carpenter smiled broadly as if she had said something that pleased him very much.

"The Great Weaver can do greater things than I can," said the Carpenter.

"Then please," pleaded Anah. "Get him for me."

"Child, you cannot *get* the Great Weaver." He said it so seriously that Anah felt she had said something as foolish as asking the Carpenter to get her the Ocean. But then he smiled again. "Child, we cannot order the Great Weaver to do anything — but we can always *ask* him — for he can help us in many different ways."

Anah, still holding on to the long length of rope that reached to the now buried shell, crossed the remaining stones and came and sat on the woodpile next to the Carpenter. Both of them stared at the lake and at the stepping stones getting smaller and smaller. The Carpenter seemed very quiet, even for a man who says very little. Then suddenly he jumped up. Anah slipped off the log she was sitting on and landed with a hard bump on the ground.

"The lake is stronger than I am," said the Carpenter. Anah remembered he had said that before. "Child, the Great Weaver has given us the lake. It has greater strength than

I have. We shall use the strength the Great Weaver has given to the lake."

Doxa and Anah both looked mystified as the Carpenter carried a small log to the sixty-third stepping stone. He then called to Anah. "Child, bring the rope."

Anah stepped on to the stones and did as she was told.

"Now," continued the Carpenter. "Pull the rope until it is tight, then tie it on to the log — but make sure you leave plenty of rope at the end. Now, push the log gently into the lake."

Anah did as she was told. The log bobbed about then drifted into the lake. The rope now reached from the shell to the bobbing log and from the log to Anah's hand.

She felt rather as if she was fishing.

"Now what do we do?" asked Anah.

"Go back to the ramp and wait," replied the Carpenter.

Anah never had been very good at waiting. Neither had Doxa. They all watched the bobbing, floating log. The tide still came in. Soon the water became so deep that the stepping stones were covered. As the water level in the lake rose, so the rope between the floating log and the stuck shell became tighter and tighter. The log floated until it was directly above the shell. The rope held fast to the flute and indeed it tightened its grip. Slowly, as the water got higher and higher, so the log pulled the rope tighter and tighter. In fact, unseen to Anah, it pulled so strongly on the shell that it slowly lifted it from the mud. Doxa, Anah and the Carpenter watched the log bob and pull and then as it made a sudden twitch, they knew something had happened. The log floated freely in the lake, with the rope hanging beneath it, and tied securely on to the end of it was the shell flute.

"The lake has pulled the shell free," said the Carpenter. "Now all you have to do is pull on the piece of rope you are holding and it will bring the log to us and then we can get the shell flute."

Anah gazed in disbelief, but pulled on the rope. It was harder than she had expected, as Doxa wanted to get a good view, but only succeeded in getting in the way. Finally, with a more than gentle push from Anah, he moved aside and Anah saw the log floating slowly towards them. As soon as she had a hold on the log Anah rolled it slightly up the ramp, so as to get at the other length of rope that hopefully stretched from the log to the shell flute. She gently tugged on the rope and, sure enough, at the surface of the water there appeared the precious shell flute. Anah danced and jumped with joy and excitement. The Royal Carpenter smiled.

"You did ... you did it," Anah cried, looking at the Carpenter.

He, in turn, looked quite horrified. "No, child, the Great Weaver did it."

Now Doxa the Carpet Dragon still wanted to see clearly what was happening. So he stood on the round log that was lying on its side just where the Princess had left it. Unfortunately as soon as he did so, it began to roll down the ramp. Doxa tried hard to keep his balance. His red, curly-toed carpet slippers moved as fast as they could as the log rolled under his feet. Faster and faster went the log as it plunged down the ramp towards the lake. Anah looked in horror as her Carpet Dragon shot past her, balanced on the top of the rolling log. Almost without thinking, she shouted out, "Doxa! Doxa! Use your wings!" She had really meant that he should use his wings to help him keep his balance, but Doxa, in total panic and because he normally did what the Princess shouted at him, spread his yellow wings and suddenly found to his horror that his feet had left the log.

It may not have been the most expert nor tidy of flights. But no one could doubt that Doxa the Carpet Dragon was flying! Anah watched in utter astonishment, clinging tightly to the shell flute, as Doxa skimmed across the lake. He flapped his wings furiously and his red curly-toed carpet slippers occasionally sent up a spray of ice-cold water. Then, much to his own amazement, he neatly wheeled around and began to head back to the Emperor's island. Now, as the tide came in, so did a fresh easterly wind from the Great Ocean. Suddenly this sea breeze caught under Doxa's furiously flapping wings and he soared high into the sky. At first he kept both red eyes tight shut. But as he realized that it was not just his wings and his effort that kept him flying — but also the wind from the Great Ocean — he began to flap his wings less energetically, and instead began to glide almost happily.

When he did return to earth, or rather to the ramp that led up to the city gates, Doxa slightly mis-timed his landing. He shot over the Princess's head straight into the remaining pile of logs that the Carpenter was neatly stacking back up.

"Goodness me," gasped the open-mouthed Princess, still holding on tight to the shell flute. "I think the Great Weaver has done something else."

And as Anah, almost without thinking, went to help re-stack the logs she was sure she heard the astonished-looking Carpenter say, "Perhaps more than you think."

Anah didn't quite understand what he meant, even though she was the Princess in the Kingdom of the Carpet Dragon.

4

The Itch-Hunt

Anah was very pleased that she had not had to use the stone that day. That evening she took her place in the banqueting hall with Doxa, next to the Emperor, for the second of the Royal Birthday celebrations.

Throughout the meal the Guardian of the Royal Treasures felt an occasional draught around his legs. He was a little surprised to find that it wasn't caused by an open door, but rather by the flapping wings of Doxa the Carpet Dragon who lay under the banqueting table.

As the oil lamp was once again lit, and a still quietness settled over the room, he leaned towards Anah and hurriedly whispered, "Have you used it yet?"

"What?" she whispered back.

"The stone," he answered.

"No, not yet," she replied.

"Oh, I just wondered," he sighed, feeling another blast of cold air from the dragon's stretched wings.

The Emperor, however, interrupted him. For everyone had finished the cakes and creams and ices that had been prepared for the celebration, and it was now time for the Princess to learn more about the Kingdom. The Emperor stood in the gentle lamplight.

"Anah. The time has come," he began. "You will now be given the second of the Royal Adviser's gifts. Tonight the Guardian of the Royal Treasures will tell you his story. It is his gift to you. It will tell you more about this Kingdom and the Great Weaver; tonight you shall hear about our sheep."

"Sheep?" interrupted Anah in a rather impolite and improper manner. For she thought she knew all there was to know about sheep! Indeed she had always regarded sheep with considerable contempt. And it seemed strange to her that a man who dealt with the most beautiful and valuable things in the Kingdom should be about to tell her about the most foolish creatures to be found.

"Yes, my most Royal Princess," answered the Guardian of the Royal Treasures in his usual hurried and breathless manner. "Sheep! Sheep are very important to us. For they give us the wool we need. Now listen carefully.

"The Great Weaver, as you know, has made many worlds. Each has its own pattern and weaves its own story." He looked up anxiously at the Emperor and Empress to ensure that he would have time to finish his story. They smiled back reassuringly.

"There was once," he hurriedly began, "a land of sheep."

"How awful," interrupted the Royal Princess, but she did not continue for she was silenced by an exceedingly long and definitely disapproving glare from the Empress.

"Yes, my most Royal Princess. A land of sheep. Perhaps I could continue, otherwise I fear we shall not have time to finish?" He paused but there was no further interruption or comments.

"Now . . . where was I? Oh yes . . . a land of sheep. Now, when this land was new and bright and in its springtime, some lambs were born and, as is the way with all young creatures . . ." he paused for a moment to ensure that the Princess was still listening, ". . . they must be taught the way of their world. So one bright morning a ewe began to teach her offspring. She told them of many things. Of how to keep sharp stones out of their feet. Of how to bleat in the seven different ways that all sheep must learn. Of the kindness of the Shepherd (for that is the name of the Great Weaver in that land), and of all that was good to eat and how the best of all food was the juicy dandelion. 'But,' she continued, 'the most important thing you must remember is the one thing a sheep must *never* do . . .'

"Now sadly, at the precise moment that the ewe began to tell her offspring about this very important thing that they must never do, a particularly plump lamb happened to notice a juicy green-stemmed plant growing immediately in front of his nose. He had heard what had been said about dandelions being the best of all food and, not unreasonably, had wondered if this might be one of those highly-to-be-desired plants. Now, being an adventurous, if not particularly polite sort of individual, he promptly poked out his tongue, wrapped it around the juicy stem and swallowed it, complete with the wispy, sneezy seeds at the top. Sadly, the ewe had failed to remind her lambs that it is essential to remove these ticklesome objects before eating the dandelion. Indeed, they proved so troublesome that our particularly plump lamb didn't hear what the ewe said about this important thing a sheep must never do. So when she repeated, 'Now will you all remember what it is that we must never do?' this particular lamb found himself nodding in agreement with all the others around him, although he had no idea what he was agreeing to.

"Now our particular lamb was not only plump, he was also rather proud. And so, whenever he heard the others bleating that they would always remember what a sheep must never do, he not only bleated the same, but he began going round advising all the other lambs about the matter. He would walk up to some poor unsuspecting creature, who was just trying to find a juicy dandelion to digest, and bleat very loudly, 'Now, do you remember what it is that a sheep must never do?'

" 'Why yes,' would always be the reply.

" 'That is very good,' he would continue in a particularly wise way.

"Now, when lambs are fed on juicy dandelion stems they soon become shaggy sheep, for their wool grows thick and heavy. By the time it was high summer our particularly shaggy sheep had become very warm and very tired. That was when he first noticed the itch on his back. Itches can be troublesome at the best of times, but this was not the best of times, nor was it an easy itch. He tried to scratch it away with each foot in turn but, although the Great Weaver had provided him with four, none of them seemed to reach. He became increasingly hot and itchy, and then he noticed a nearby tree with attractively rough bark.

" 'Baaa!' sighed our shaggy sheep in the first and happy sort of way that all sheep are taught to bleat.

"But no one heard, except for the sharp-eared, long-tongued wolf that lived nearby. And our sheep didn't notice him.

" 'Just the thing for a troublesome itch,' continued the shaggy sheep as he set off to be rid of his wretchedness. The others watched at a distance and, thinking that this particular sheep was wise beyond his years, they decided to follow. What they saw was their dearest brother trying to stand on his two back legs and rub his back against a rough, tough tree. So when he moved away, the others tried to copy the performance, believing it must be a particularly wise thing to do. The truth was that the itch had not been remedied, but this particularly wise sheep had now noticed a low branch on a nearby prickly bush.

" 'Baaa!' whispered our woolly sheep in the second and cunning sort of way that all sheep are taught to bleat.

"But no one heard, except for the sharp-eared, long-tongued wolf that sat nearby. And our sheep didn't notice him.

" 'If I were to walk under that prickly branch my itch would be no more,' continued the woolly sheep. However, when he got closer to the bush, he saw that it was much larger than his eyes had led him to believe, and that the prickly branch was so high that he couldn't reach it at all. He tried jumping up to scratch his back. But even though he was a particularly energetic jumper, he still could not scratch his back. He left the others to copy the strange behaviour of their particular hero, for now he thought he saw the very thing. Down in the valley there hubbled and bubbled a shimmering stream. And by it there was a patch of crunchy gravel.

" 'Baaa!' exclaimed our excited sheep in the third and wise sort of way that all sheep are taught to bleat.

"But no one heard, except for the sharp-eared, long-tongued wolf that watched nearby. And our sheep didn't notice him.

"And so without further ado he set out at once for the gravelly stream, with the others following at a respectable distance.

"When he arrived at the crunchy gravel, he knew what was to be done to relieve the relentless itch. So he lay down on one side.

The crunchy gravel scratched at his shaggy fleece and then with wonderful relief he rolled on to his back.

" 'Baaa!' gasped our gigglesome sheep in the fourth and silly sort of way that all sheep are taught to bleat.

"But no one heard, except for the sharp-eared, long-tongued wolf that hid nearby. And our sheep didn't notice him.

"For he was enjoying this scratchy gravel too much, and would no doubt have remained in this sublime state had not the others in his family arrived. They gazed at him in sheepish shock. Some stood open-mouthed while others bleated in panic.

" 'Baaa!' snapped our squirming sheep in the fifth and irritated sort of way that all sheep are taught to bleat. But no one heard, for the others weren't listening; they all thought they could smell a sharp-eared, long-tongued wolf crouching nearby.

" 'Anyway,' continued our squirming sheep, thoroughly enjoying himself. 'It's very good.' And he crunched the scratchy gravel delightfully into his itchy wool.

" 'But look at you,' bleated a small, shocked voice. 'Why, you're on your back! You've done what a sheep must never do!'

" 'I have?' came the surprised reply from the mystified upside-down sheep.

" 'Yes, you have,' came a chorus of bewildered bleats in all the first five ways that sheep are taught to bleat. 'For a sheep must *never* roll on his back. Surely you know that. Our mother told us that.'

" 'And the Shepherd said so,' continued a frail, thin lamb.

" 'Baaa?' questioned our quizzical sheep in the sixth and rather rude sort of way that all sheep are taught to bleat. But no one heard, for the others weren't listening; they all saw the sharp-eared, long-tongued wolf that stood nearby.

"All, that is, except our particular sheep, who could see very little as he was still upside-down.

"And so he continued, 'Oh, the Shepherd said so, did he? Well that's because the Shepherd doesn't want us to have any fun and because . . .' But our particular sheep never finished. For at that moment even he saw the sharp-eared, long-tongued wolf, who interrupted and slobbered, 'And it was also very foolish to roll on your back. For you . . . O wise and woolly one . . . will never get back onto your feet!'

"Now some of the sheep began to shake alarmingly. Their fleeces quivered from the tips of their flat noses to the ends of their short tails. For, not unreasonably, they feared the sharp-eared, long-tongued wolf more than anything.

"But our particular sheep was not only foolish, he was also, in his own way, quite brave. He knew that he was, for a sheep, quite strong, and could run quite fast when the need arose. And he had a definite feeling, even though he was upside-down, that perhaps the need had arisen.

" 'Of course I can get on my feet,' he exclaimed, expecting simply to roll over and scamper off before the wolf could so much as wink one of his cruel eyes.

"But sadly, unlike our particular sheep, the sharp-eared wolf *had* heard what it was that a sheep must never do. And so, when our foolishly floundering sheep tried to roll over and found that the springiness in his wool simply pushed him back, it was not the sharp-eared, long-tongued wolf that was surprised. Our shocked sheep tried to roll backwards and forwards, and from side to side, so as to find his feet again, but always his shaggy fleece returned him to his peculiar position.

"For the simple truth was that he could not get up.

" 'And now, wise one,' slobbered the sharp-eared, long-tongued wolf, 'you must wait until night falls when the cruel pecking crows go looking for foolish sheep — and then I shall return for you!'

"The wolf slunk away with an awful grin and a slobbering snigger.

"Some of the other sheep ran away in terror. Others came to reassure him that the crows would most certainly come once it was dark, and they gave him all manner of suggestions as to how he might fight them off. And even though our particular sheep knew he was strong, he also realized that there was little he could do with all his four feet pointing at the stars.

"Others bleated how sad they were to have trusted and respected such a foolish sheep, and how he now deserved to meet with the sharp-eared, long-tongued wolf.

"One did try to help. But then he remembered that crunchy gravel was bad for a sheep's feet, and so he, too, soon left.

"By the time the sun was setting, our particular sheep was all alone. He knew that he had been very foolish, and he wished that he had been honest. For now he was the saddest and most frightened sheep in all that land. Then it was that he found the strength to bleat in the seventh and saddest sort of way that all sheep are taught to bleat. That is a very strong sort of bleat, but, even so, no one heard. For the other sheep would not listen and the sharp-eared, long-tongued wolf was too busy preparing for his supper. But the seventh bleat is very powerful and can be heard very far away. And at last our particular sheep's seventh bleat was heard — by the Shepherd himself. The Shepherd knew all the bleats of his sheep. And so he came to the crunchy scratchy gravel and saw the upside-down sheep.

"As soon as he saw that sad and sorrowful sheep he knew what had happened. But he was not angry, even with a sheep that was so foolish and disobedient. For he truly cared, and loved those sheep. Strangely, he seemed as sad as the sheep was. The Shepherd said nothing — but walked over the crunchy gravel and knelt down beside the sheep.

"And the sheep felt the Shepherd's strong hands push at his sides and pull at his wool, and then he felt the gravel once again under his feet and he knew he had been saved from becoming supper for a sharp-eared, long-tongued wolf.

"For, my most Royal Princess, the Shepherd, or the Great Weaver, as we know him, had a very different plan in store for that particular woolly sheep. And it is a very good thing that he did."

The Guardian of the Royal Treasures paused for a moment and looked into the wide dark eyes of the Princess, to make sure that she was still listening.

"For some say that because that particular woolly sheep found the strength to bleat in the powerful seventh and sorrowful sort of way, instead of ending up as a wolf's supper, he was brought by the Great Weaver to our land. And they even say that he became one of the distant ancestors of all the shaggy sheep in our Kingdom."

The Princess didn't doubt this for a moment, for all the sheep she had ever seen were very shaggy and also remarkably foolish.

"And as you know," continued the Guardian of the Royal Treasures, "without those shaggy sheep we would have no wool, and without their thick wool we could weave no carpets, and without those wonderfully woven carpets we would have no wealth to share." There was a long silence, until the Emperor himself spoke gently.

"And so, Anah, whenever we look at the sheep in our land we will remember how very foolish some creatures can be when they will not listen to others. But that the Great Weaver still cares about even the most foolish of them. And that a Princess of this Kingdom must care for them and love them as well."

But Anah had stopped listening. Instead she was looking again at the Emperor's stone that she held in her hand. For, to be honest, she cared more about the stone than about sheep, even though she was a Princess in the Kingdom of the Carpet Dragon.

5

The Fire-Key

The Princess of the Kingdom of the Carpet Dragon was woken by the sound of sneezing. It was Doxa the Carpet Dragon who was making the strange snorting sound. He had been sleeping in the doorway to the Princess's bedroom and had been dreaming that he was a real fire-breathing dragon. He was just about to take a deep breath to snort fire at a pirate ship that kept appearing in his dreams, when he suddenly woke up with the sneezes. A small feather from the Princess's quilted eiderdown had tickled his nose.

The Princess decided that she could not go back to sleep and so she got up and dressed. She was not in a particularly good mood. For one thing she was still tired; for another she was a little worried that she had still not used the stone to change something.

She realized now that it might take a little longer than she had first thought to find something really important to change. But she was sure that it would be worth the wait, for who knew what would happen when she eventually used the stone? Clearly the stone must have tremendous power – and maybe its power would last longer than the Empress had said. Anyway, what did she really know about such things?

Now although unpredictable, this particular Royal Princess could at times be surprisingly practical. She decided to search for whatever it was that she would change in a very orderly way. She would start in the Palace, then look throughout the city. Then, if need be, she would cross over the stepping stones and look among the trees that grew along the lakeside. She might even climb one of the hills where the shaggy sheep grazed. For Anah thought she could remember being told something about the stone working as long as she could still see the island. Sadly, although the Princess could be practical, she could also be rather forgetful.

She could also be rather careless, and she didn't want to risk losing the stone as she had lost the shell flute. So she decided it would be wise to keep the Emperor's gift safe until she found a use for it. She could soon return and collect it. But where could she keep it for safety? Anah looked around the room, and she saw her money-box. It was shaped like a dragon. Doxa had always thought that it looked a very fine dragon indeed, for it had a wide open mouth with fire breathing from it and it was made from pure silver. It was also quite hollow and had a small slit in the mouth through which Anah could drop coins, and a little wooden trap-door in the base to get them out again. Now this wooden trap-door had a tiny lock on it which could be opened and closed with a flat, silver key. Anah had never actually managed to fill the dragon money-box with coins, so there was always plenty of room inside it for other precious objects.

Now Anah decided that this would be the ideal place to keep the Emperor's gift. But it would obviously not be wise to let too many people know where the gift was to be kept. Of course, she trusted Doxa, but she also liked secrets. So Anah decided that not even Doxa the Carpet Dragon should know where the Emperor's gift was to be hidden. Suddenly an idea seemed to drop into her mind.

"Doxa! Did you hear that?"

Doxa, who was still sneezing, pricked up his ears. He had heard nothing, but then he trusted his ears about as much as he trusted his tail.

"I'm sure I heard something down the passageway," continued the Princess. "Quickly!

Go and see for me. It might be some disaster and then we can use the stone."

Without a moment's hesitation Doxa shot out of the room and charged down the corridor. As soon as he was gone, the Princess lifted up the dragon money-box, opened the wooden base and carefully dropped the Emperor's gift inside, for it was too large to be dropped through the slit in the mouth. She then locked the wooden trap-door at the bottom and put the small, silver key in her pocket.

Meanwhile Doxa the Carpet Dragon thought he had found a disaster. Sadly it turned out to be only the Guardian of the Royal Treasures, hurrying down to the Emperor's vault.

Doxa soon realized his mistake. One of the advantages of running around a stone-floored palace in curly-toed carpet slippers is that you can't be heard. But the disadvantage is that you can't stop either. Doxa wasn't heard and he couldn't stop. The poor Guardian of the Royal Treasures was carrying a beautifully decorated china vase that had just been given to the Emperor. He was never really sure what it was that bowled him over and, indeed, he was so busy juggling with the precious pot, that he didn't have time to look. But he was sure that he saw for a moment the pointed purple tail of a Carpet Dragon flick into view. "Drat that dragon's tail," he sighed, but Doxa hadn't heard, for he had decided to return quickly to the Princess's room. He stood behind the door puffing and panting in the way that Carpet Dragons do.

"Oh, you poor thing," commented the Princess, without even looking up at the dragon. "It must have been something else I heard." Doxa didn't doubt that she was right. "I know. You stay here while I go and look around the Palace on my own." The Princess had decided that she might be more successful on her own and, should she need it, she could soon return and collect the Emperor's gift. She had turned to leave the room when she heard a faint tinkling sound at her feet. Anah looked down and saw the small silver key. She felt in her pocket and discovered a little hole through which she stuck a finger. Instantly it turned into a big hole.

"Oh no," she muttered. But really she was quite pleased to have found the hole. Supposing she had lost the dragon money-box key while on her search? Clearly she would now have to find somewhere for the key. Where could she put it to be safe while she was gone? She thought for a moment. Then another bright idea seemed to drop into her mind. She went to a drawer and found a

piece of bright red wool, which she tied to the silver key.

"Now Doxa. Listen carefully. This is most precious. I want you to look after it while I'm gone and keep it very safe." And with that she hung the key around the dragon's neck.

Now Doxa was quite pleased that he would not have to go on another adventure, but he was even more pleased to have a silver key hung around his neck. He looked down at it, and by the time he looked up again Anah had gone. He was very proud to be trusted with such a precious object, even though he had no idea what it was. But then he began to think what would happen if *he* were to lose it and he began to doubt that he could look after it properly. He suddenly felt very lonely. All this responsibility was definitely worrying. In desperation he began to look around the room for somewhere safe to put the key. Now, where did the Princess put precious things? Then suddenly he saw the silver dragon money-box.

"Of course," he thought and went over to it. The key was very flat, and it slipped through the slit in the mouth of the silver dragon money-box with incredible ease. Doxa tried to poke the wool in behind it but it got wedged in the slit and, no matter how hard he tried, he couldn't poke the bright red wool through.

He looked at the blocked slit and decided that the key would be safe enough anyway.

Then he went to lie down on the Princess's bed, exhausted, but pleased that he had done so well.

Meanwhile Anah was searching for something important to change. Twice she thought she had found something. The first was when she saw one of the royal dogs going round and round in circles on three legs. It looked so pitiful and sad that Anah almost went to collect the Emperor's gift straightaway, she so much wanted to change the dog's misery and make it well again. But then she wondered if even this was the best use for the stone. She was about to call for one of the Royal Dog Handlers, when she decided that she could do something herself. The poor creature had apparently been trying to scratch behind its left ear and a back paw had got stuck in its collar. Although the creature growled and snarled with fear and frustration as she approached, she went and calmed it down and freed its trapped leg. She felt strangely pleased with herself — the same feeling she'd had when she had managed to get the shell back.

"Well, there was obviously no need to use the stone there," she said. And she set out again. She went into the Royal Kitchens and was more than a little surprised to find the Royal Cook in deep despair and sorrow over some pies. He hadn't made enough pastry to put lids on the pies for that night's Royal Birthday celebrations and there wasn't enough flour to make any more. The poor man was weeping so bitterly that Anah was quite worried he would spoil the pastry that he did have.

"I know. I'll use the stone," thought Anah. "I can change things so that all the cooking will be done and all the pies made. Then the cook will be pleased and everyone will enjoy the Royal Birthday. This is definitely it. I'll get the stone straightaway." But then she stopped and thought again. True, she could use the stone to change things. But there might be something else she could do. She didn't want to waste the Emperor's gift. Suddenly one of those bright ideas just popped into her mind again.

"I know!" she exclaimed. "Why don't we put a dollop of cream on top of each of the pies. They'll look much nicer."

The cook was delighted with the idea and was more than a little surprised when Anah herself began to help him. They had great fun, and Anah was pleased that the cook was happy once more.

Anah returned to her room, pleased with what she had done.

Now Anah was not particularly quiet when she walked down the stone corridor even with curly-toed carpet slippers on. Doxa heard her coming and quickly jumped off the bed. Anah hardly noticed the fluffy dent on her feather eiderdown where her dragon had been sleeping. But she did notice that the dragon was no longer wearing the precious key.

"Doxa, where have you put the key I gave you?" She was trying to sound calm but she gradually turned very pale. "No one has taken it, have they?"

Doxa jumped up. He flipped his tail in delight and went over to the dragon money-box. He picked it up. Anah saw the tell-tale piece of red wool blocking the mouth of the dragon and realized at once what had happened. She grabbed the money-box and tried to prise the wool out of the slit. But Doxa had done a very good job of jamming it tightly and neatly in the silver dragon's mouth. She tried shaking the dragon money-box, but was worried that she might damage the Emperor's gift. She was, to say the least, furious.

"You stupid, silly, foolish, fluffy dragon!" she shouted. "You've got no more sense than a sheep!" She also shouted lots of other things; some of them were very unkind and most of them were not true.

Doxa just stood there. He wanted to hide, but normally when he hid it was *in* his Princess's room. He couldn't think where else to go. So he just lay down. It wouldn't have hurt so much had the Princess pulled his tail. She didn't. But the things she said caused him real pain. For Anah never really knew how much a Carpet Dragon could understand, nor how much he could be hurt. Doxa's misery was total and complete. He doubted if he had ever felt worse. It seemed as if something very cold had happened inside him and it certainly didn't help when the Princess sneered, "Now I suppose I shall never be able to change anything in this Kingdom — simply because *you* don't listen to what I tell you or do what you're told!" Which wasn't really true, for the gift was still quite safe, and no one had taken it. It was just that the furious Princess couldn't get at it. Then Doxa found things did get worse. For Anah stopped shouting at the Carpet Dragon and started ignoring him. She moved around her room as if he simply didn't exist.

Anah, although very angry, was also rather worried. How could she get the stone back with the key inside the money-box? She could of course go and ask her father, for she was sure that he would be able to help but, strangely, when she was angry she never felt like asking for his help. She wouldn't have listened to anything he said, anyway.

She even thought of asking the Great Weaver for help. She didn't doubt that he could help her – but, if the truth were known, she felt rather guilty for the way she had treated Doxa and didn't really feel like talking to the Great Weaver. Then she decided that that was ridiculous. Doxa was only a Carpet Dragon after all and, if the Great Weaver wanted to help her, he could do so without her having to ask him! Then suddenly she had another bright idea. The Guardian of the Royal Treasures should know about locks and things. Surely he could help?' So she went down to the Royal Treasury.

She found him unlocking the huge gates to the Emperor's treasures in the royal vault. He was getting the blue-and-white china vase out again. Apparently the Emperor had found someone to give it to. The Emperor was always giving treasures away. The Guardian of the Royal Treasures held the vase in one hand and a huge key in the other. The Royal Princess quickly explained what had happened.

"Well, I'm sorry, Princess. I really don't think I can help. There is only one key that the Emperor has and that is this one." He

held up the large key. "Some say that the
Great Weaver himself designed it for, if you
look carefully, the handle is in the shape of
a sheep and, as I said yesterday . . ."

"Well, that's all very well," interrupted
Anah in a rather irritated way, for she had
no intention of listening to him, "but it's
not going to open this lock, is it?" And she
looked at the huge key and then again at the
tiny lock in her money-box.

"I'm sorry, Princess, but this is the only
key the Emperor has."

Anah stamped away in a most rude manner and returned to her room. She was frus-
trated and more than a little exhausted. It's
surprising how being angry tires you out.
Indeed, unless you are very determined, it's
difficult to be angry for long. In the end you
stop being angry and simply start sulking.

Anah was just beginning to enjoy a really
good sulk. She looked at the money-box
that she held in her hands and then she
saw Doxa looking about as sad, miserable
and pathetic as a dragon can. In fact he had
rolled over on to his back and was lying
quite still, which is a thing that dragons do
if they are really miserable or frightened.
To start with, it irritated her and made her
want to be even more unkind, but for some
reason it also reminded her of something.

She couldn't think what it was – and then she remembered. It was the foolish sheep from the story of the night before. The more she looked at Doxa the more she remembered. And she began to wish that she hadn't listened to that story — for she began to feel very uncomfortable. She knew how differently she had treated Doxa compared with the way the Great Weaver treated the foolish sheep. And then she began to feel sad, too. A true, deep sadness.

She didn't feel sad because she couldn't get the stone.

She didn't even feel sad because of what she had done and said to Doxa.

No, she felt sad simply because Doxa looked so miserable and helpless. For she realized she did care about him, and she did love him. All at once she found herself kneeling beside the desperate Carpet Dragon. She didn't quite know what she was going to do. Perhaps she was going to try to roll Doxa over as the Great Weaver had rolled the foolish sheep. She didn't know why. Perhaps that might make him feel a bit better.

She put the metal money-box down in front of Doxa but, as she went to push him over, she found that she was giving him a hug and saying, "Oh Doxa, I'm sorry. I know you were only trying to help. I don't want you to be so sad. I do care about you. I do love you.'' And suddenly it didn't seem a silly thing to say or do to a dragon, even a Carpet Dragon. It seemed the right thing. And so it was. For something else happened. As she said that she still cared about the dragon and loved him, the cold feeling inside Doxa melted and a very warm feeling took its place.

Now that was a good thing, but Doxa, although only a Carpet Dragon, was none the less a real dragon. So the warmth inside Doxa began to come out. In fact, it blew out — down his nose. Doxa had never breathed fire before and, to be honest, it wasn't really fire that he breathed now. It was more like warm air. Very warm air indeed.

Now Anah had left her metal money-box right in front of Doxa's nose, so when the blast of warm air came, the money-box was right in the way. Suddenly the money-box got very hot indeed. So hot that the air inside tried to rush out like the steam from a kettle. But there was no way for it to get out for the base was locked and the mouth was blocked. The air inside the silver dragon became hotter and hotter until suddenly, with a loud pop, the wooden trap-door in the base of the metal dragon burst open. The hot air rushed out and the Emperor's Royal Birthday gift rolled onto the floor.

Anah reached out for her gift in total surprise and then leaped around the room with joy. She didn't know if she was so happy because she had the stone back — or because Doxa, her Carpet Dragon, had breathed fire — well, nearly fire.

"Oh Doxa . . . how did you do that?"

Doxa didn't really know. He was very pleased anyway.

The Princess was also pleased that she had listened to the story of the foolish sheep. She stopped and thought for a moment and sighed, "Do you know, I think the Great Weaver helped me again."

She turned to see if Doxa was listening. But he was lost in a cloud of smoke that had just drifted contentedly from his nose. Anah didn't mind at all, even if she was the Princess in the Kingdom of the Carpet Dragon.

6

The Bird-King

Anah was pleased that she had not used the stone that day. Particularly when she heard everyone agreeing that the cream-topped pies were the very best that they had ever eaten in the Kingdom, and that they were without a doubt the high spot so far of the third evening's Royal Birthday festivities. Once again, as it grew dark, the smoky oil lamps were lit and a still quietness settled over the room. In the dim light the Keeper of the Royal Diary leaned slightly towards Anah and whispered to the wide-eyed child,

"Have you used it yet?"

"What?" she whispered back.

"The stone," he answered solemnly.

"No, not yet," she replied.

"Oh, I just wondered," he sighed, watching another puff of smoke drift up from the sleeping Carpet Dragon who lay at her feet.

The Emperor, however, had risen to his feet. And Anah knew it was now time for her to learn more about the Kingdom. In fact, she was now eager to learn more about her Kingdom. So when the Emperor said, "Anah, it is now time for the third of the Royal Adviser's gifts," Anah smiled enthusiastically. "Tonight the Keeper of the Royal Diary will tell you his story. It is his gift to you. It, too, will tell you more about this Kingdom and the Great Weaver, for he will tell you about the sixty-six stepping stones."

Anah looked back at the Keeper of the Royal Diary. She quite liked the tall thin man, but he was a rather serious sort of person and his face was always solemn, and he very rarely smiled. He bowed low to the Emperor, straightened himself then, much to Anah's surprise, he suddenly bowed low to her as well. Indeed, so sudden was his movement, that his beautifully embroidered dome-shaped cap shot off his head and landed on the Guardian of the Royal Treasures' cream-topped cake. The poor man lifted the dome-shaped cap out of his cream-topped cake and mumbled that at least it wasn't a dragon's tail. He passed the object back to the Keeper of the Royal Diary.

Doxa opened one red eye, looked up at the mumbling figure, and puffed a large and rather noisy cloud of smoke. Meanwhile, the Keeper of the Royal Diary returned the sticky cap to his head and tried to look as solemn as normal. Anah tried not to smile.

"Princess," he began in a very serious manner with a blob of cream dripping like an icicle from the side of his cap. "The Great Weaver has made many worlds." He solemnly shook his head, which made the blob of cream drop on to his left ear. "And each of them has its own pattern and weaves its own story.

"There was once a land with a deep, dark forest."

The room seemed to grow a little darker as the sombre voice of the Keeper of the Royal Diary continued. "And in that deep, dark forest there was a lake with just one rock in it." The Princess's eyes widened and her mouth opened. Clearly this was going to be a very serious story.

"Now in that land there were many animals. Each of them thought it was the most important — so they often argued with one another. But it was the birds that fought most. The poor things were always arguing, so that the Great Weaver had to give them a judge to sort out their squabbles. That judge was the gentle dove.

"Now, one day, three of the most squabblesome and important birds met at the side of the lake. As they stood, they argued as to which bird in the forest should be the King of the Birds. It was very sad."

Doxa, who had woken up for the story, looked at the Keeper of the Royal Diary's solemn face and didn't doubt for one moment just how very sad it was.

"For," continued the sombre voice, "they had no need of a king. The Great Weaver had already sent the dove to rule over them.

" 'Well,' quacked the duck. 'I think the King of the Birds should be a duck.' And she slapped her flippy floppy webbed foot on the ground to show how strongly she felt about it.

" 'Nonsense,' squawked the crow. 'It must be a crow.'

" 'No, no,' hooted the owl. 'It must be a wise bird, not you . . . but an owl.' And he looked at them with his huge eyes.

"The discussion was about to develop into a really serious argument when suddenly, on the rock in the middle of the lake, there appeared a strange creature that none of them had ever seen before.

" 'Caw,' cried the crow in surprise. 'What are you?'

"The strange creature made no reply for, in all honesty, it didn't seem to know.

" 'How odd,' quacked the duck. 'Just look at its feet. Why, the beautiful creature has feet like mine!' And she looked down at her large flippy floppy webbed feet. 'And everyone knows that truly important birds have webbed feet.' She bent down to look at the scraggly feet of her two companions and then continued, 'This creature that has suddenly appeared must be a really important bird to have feet like that.'

"The strange creature on the rock seemed to understand, for it spoke up in a rasping, croaking, cawing squawk.

The crow, who was, of course, just about to disagree with the duck, stopped and listened to the sound, his head tilted slightly to one side so as to hear more fully.

" 'Caw ... you might actually be right, duck! Did you hear its voice? Why, it's got a voice like mine. And everyone knows that a truly important bird would have a voice like that.' He waited to hear what the duck had to say — but she had decided not to use her voice.

"The owl, who was getting a little concerned about the strange creature, peered across the lake and was astonished to see that the strange creature also had two huge black eyes which it used to stare back with.

" 'Two eyes,' he hooted. 'Look at its two eyes. Why, it too has two eyes like mine. And we all know that *troooly* important birds have two eyes like my two huge eyes. You two were right when you said this is a truly important bird.'

"Now it so happened that the Great Weaver's dove was flying through the deep, dark wood when it came upon the three birds and the strange creature. It stopped high in a tree to listen to what was happening.

" 'Caw!' squawked the crow in total surprise. 'We seem to have agreed.'

" 'Yes, we have,' quacked the duck.

" 'Too true,' hooted the owl.

" 'This creature must be a very important bird,' continued the crow. 'In fact, if it has all of our good points, it must be such a great bird that it might even be the King of the Birds.'

" 'The King, the King!' quacked the duck, flapping her flippy floppy webbed feet excitedly in the mud.

" 'Too true, the King,' hooted the owl.

" 'Caw, we have a King!' squawked the crow, his loud voice echoing through the deep, dark forest, so that every other bird could hear.

"Now the dove, who was wiser than any other creature in that land, knew that this was not the King of the Birds and decided that she would have to do something before a disaster took place. She flew down amongst the three birds that were busy bowing to their new King across the lake. They all saw her coming.

" 'Caw . . . what do you want?' squawked the crow.

" 'Who asked you to come here?' hooted the owl.

" 'Yes,' continued the quacking duck. 'We don't need you any more. We have a new king now. In fact . . . you're not wanted at all.'

"All of this hardly ruffled the gentle feathers of the dove, who simply answered, 'Perhaps I am not wanted, but I may be needed. This creature cannot truly be your king.'

" 'Caw . . . why not?' interrupted the crow.

" 'Yes, why not?' flapped the duck. 'You're just jealous.'

" 'Too true,' sneered the hooting owl.

"The dove bowed her head graciously. She was clearly saddened but had no intention of giving up her task.

" 'I can see,' she continued after a short pause, 'that you are all wise birds.'

"The three creatures before her remained unusually silent, each one waiting for another to disagree. 'And indeed,' she continued, 'you are all important birds.' There was another pause until the owl hooted in agreement.

" 'Too true, too true.'

" 'Then,' continued the gentle dove, 'perhaps you have been looking at the wrong things. You seem to think that a truly great bird has only those things that make you *different* from each other. Surely, if you are all important birds, a truly great bird would have those things that make you the same.'

"There was a very long silence while each of the three birds thought deeply. It was the owl that first agreed.

" 'Too true,' he hooted. 'Too true.' Then the others all agreed.

" 'Oh good,' cooed the dove with obvious satisfaction. 'Then can we agree that all of you have feathers and wings and can fly?'

" 'Caw . . .' cried the crow without hesitation. 'You are right, you know.'

" 'Y-Yes, I did know,' continued the dove without the slightest hint of pride. 'But I am so pleased that you agree with me.' The other three birds nodded their approval. 'Well, then,' continued the cooing dove. 'Surely a truly great bird must at least have feathers, wings, and be able to fly?' She said this in such a gentle and matter-of-fact way that they all instantly agreed. 'Well, come with me and let's look more closely at your chosen king.'

"The three birds all quickly preened their feathers, stretched their wings and were very careful to fly across to the rock in the middle of the lake.

" 'Well,' continued the dove, standing a little apart from the other three birds. 'Does your king have feathers?'

" 'Quack! No!' flapped the duck. 'It's got slimy skin. Yuk.' And she flapped away from the strange creature in disgust.

" 'Well then, does it have wings?' gently cooed the dove.

" 'No, no, it has tiny front legs. No wings, no,' reassured the hooting, preening owl.

" 'Well then, perhaps it can fly?' interrupted the dove.

" 'Caw . . .' cried the crow. 'Of course it can fly. Just look at it.'

"But the poor creature made no attempt to move. So the crow gave it an encouraging peck. It jumped high into the air with a loud cry and then hopped and flopped across the rock until it plopped into the water of the lake. Clearly it could not fly. The three birds were very disappointed.

" 'I'm sorry that you were nearly wrong,' cooed the dove sadly.

" 'Nearly wrong?' quacked the duck questioningly.

" 'Oh yes,' cried the dove. 'You weren't

97

completely wrong, for that creature was a king.'

" 'Caw . . . a king?' cried the crow. 'That thing's a king? But it can't even fly!'

" 'No, but it is still a king,' reassured the dove. 'For that is the first frog in this land.'

" 'Anyway,' quacked the duck, waddling away. 'I never said it was the King of the Birds. It was you two who made that silly suggestion.'

" 'Us two . . . what do you mean?' hooted the owl. 'It was you two!'

" 'Caw . . . rubbish,' cried the crow. 'Anyway, who said the dove was right? It might have been a bird — but perhaps it was the worst bird in the land.'

" 'Yes,' quacked the duck. 'Maybe that's it. It's the worst bird.'

" 'True, true,' hooted the owl as they all three continued their foolish discussions.

"The dove listened with great sadness, but as she listened she also watched the frog as it hopped and flopped its way across the lake. And, being wise, she remembered it had taken sixty-six hops and flops to reach the other side, and she told this to the Great Weaver himself.

"And Princess," continued the Keeper of the Royal Diary in a very serious manner, "some say that it is a good thing that she did so, for, strangely, when the Great Weaver wove our land, he made it with sixty-six stepping stones to reach across the lake to the Emperor's city."

There was a long silence while the Keeper of the Royal Diary solemnly sat down and got on with the serious business of wiping the cream from his left ear. Meanwhile the Emperor himself spoke quietly to the slightly puzzled Princess.

"You see, Anah," he began, "the Great Weaver wanted to remind us that whenever anyone crosses over the stepping stones to visit this Palace where you will one day rule, they must be seen in the right way. For all of us are different. But it is not the differences that matter. It is what makes us all the *same* that is truly important. We are all made by the Great Weaver and each one of us matters to him."

As another puff of smoke drifted from Doxa's nose, the Emperor looked deeply into Anah's dark and sleepy eyes and smiled kindly at the Princess of the Kingdom of the Carpet Dragon.

7

The Boat-Tail

The Princess of the Kingdom of the Carpet
Dragon woke early. She had slept very
deeply and had dreamed about the Emperor's gift. She sighed and looked at the
Carpet Dragon, sleeping peacefully as usual
at her bedroom door. She wondered what
he dreamed about. She watched as Doxa
stretched his wings, puffed a small cloud
of steamy smoke and then lifted his tail
high into the air, swished it to the left and
the right and let it fall back down. Unfortunately he had lifted it so high that as it fell
the flat, pointed end smacked down on his
nose and a sudden puff of smoke appeared
from under it. Doxa opened one red eye. The
flat, pointed end of his tail covered the other
eye like a floppy cap. The Princess looked
in amazement at her Carpet Dragon and
thought for a moment that Doxa reminded
her of the Keeper of the Royal Diary. She
smiled widely and muttered, "Whatever
goes on in your head?"

In fact Doxa, the flying, smoke-breathing Carpet Dragon, had been dreaming that his tail behaved itself. That it did what every other animal's tail in the Kingdom seemed to do, which was simply follow behind its owner. But Doxa's tail didn't seem to work that way. Even when he was asleep! And he doubted that it ever would.

The Princess and her dragon set out for another day of adventure, trying to find a use for the stone. She was now convinced that somewhere there was something that she alone could change. Why the Emperor had chosen her to do it, she couldn't guess. But the searching had made her Royal Birthday an occasion to remember.

She set out again with Doxa and searched for some time in the lofty, tapestry-hung rooms of the Royal Palace — but found nothing to change — other than the fact that all this searching made her hungry. So breakfast took longer than usual. It was while she was eating her third bowl of porridge that the Empress told Anah that the fourth day of the Princess's Royal Birthday celebration was to be a special day of festivities in the Kingdom. Everyone in the city had been invited by the Emperor to come to watch a boat race around the Emperor's island. And, as a very special treat, the Princess herself could take part.

She would be in one of the boats.

The Princess was delighted for, like every-one else who lived in the Emperor's city, she loved boats. But the Emperor had never allowed her to take part in the races that were held on special occasions until she had learned to swim. She had spent many hours in the cold waters of the lake before she had finally managed to satisfy the Royal Tutors that she could, in fact, swim. Even then she wasn't really sure they believed her. By then their long scrolls explaining exactly how to swim had become so wet that they fell apart. So the two tutors, not knowing what else to do, pronounced that the Princess *could* swim.

The boat races were to be held that very afternoon, which meant that she only had the morning to find a use for the stone.

Doxa and his Princess searched every-where in the Emperor's Palace, from the topmost towers to the cold, damp cellars. She was now very good at finding small things to change – things that really didn't need her to use her gift, but which she could change without wasting the power of the stone. Indeed, she decided she really would have to change such things, just to avoid having to use the stone.

So when the Carpenter lost a saw, it was Anah who found it for him under some wood shavings in the corner of his room.

"Mmm," he said in astonished but thankful appreciation, but before he could continue, the end of Doxa's tail had suddenly decided to flip into a pot of glue that the Carpenter had been using. Glue splattered the Carpenter's apron.

"Mmm," came the most disapproving sigh from the huge man, and there were no further thanks from the Carpenter.

Later the Guardian of the Royal Treasures had needed some help to find some gold rings that the Emperor wanted to give away. Anah found them. They were in a silver teapot.

"Why, that is most unusually helpful of you, Princess," he had begun to say. And she was quite sure that he was going to say something else pleasant about her, if Doxa's tail had not decided at that precise moment to flop down and flatten one of the poor man's curly-toed carpet slippers. (And, of course, his foot which was, not surprisingly, still in it.)

"Oh drat that dragon's tail," he gasped. "I don't know what the Great Weaver ever gave it to him for," and, holding his throbbing foot, he hopped around the Royal Treasury and said nothing more to her.

The Princess was beginning to be a little irritated by Doxa's unmanageable tail.

And so, by the time they had helped the Collector of the Royal Books mend some torn pages in a valuable picture book, and Doxa's tail had got wrapped up in the sticky tape, and the Collector of the Royal Books had said that the Kingdom would be better off without such irritating tails, the Princess had begun to get very cross indeed with Doxa.

But it was when they met the Keeper of the Royal Diary that she finally exploded. He was miserably shaking his solemn head and sighing deeply that he would not be able to keep an accurate account in the Kingdom's diary of that afternoon's boat race because he had run out of ink. Anah said that she had some in her room, and that he might borrow it. She had run off with Doxa to collect it, leaving the open-mouthed, astonished man waiting in disbelief for the Princess's return. For he had never known the Princess to be so helpful before. However, when she did return, it was with only half a bottle of ink, and a very miserable-looking Carpet Dragon with an incredibly inky tail trailing behind. The Keeper of the Royal Diary shook his head solemnly and suggested that, once and for

all, something ought to be done to that dragon's menacing tail. Suddenly Anah couldn't stand the sight of Doxa's tail.

"Doxa," she yelled in an incredibly loud voice. "I am fed up with your tail. Why can't it behave like everyone else's tail? Why does your tail have to be different?"

Doxa thought that this was a little unfair, as he had noticed that the Princess didn't have to cope with a tail at all. But she hadn't finished yet. Indeed she had only just begun to explain what she felt about his tail.

"Do you know," she blasted. "We would all be much better off if you didn't have a tail at all. In fact *you* would be better off. I've a very good mind to use my birthday stone to get rid of your tail. That would really change things, because your tail causes the greatest problems in the whole of this Kingdom."

The Keeper of the Royal Diary shook his head solemnly in agreement. Doxa felt most miserable.

In fact Anah had no intention of using the stone for such a thing. Indeed, she didn't really know if the stone would work like that. But Doxa was worried. He knew his tail was unpredictable, and perhaps it did cause trouble, but he was very attached to it and would really miss it if it weren't there. He really quite liked the way the Great Weaver had made him — if only his tail could be more trustworthy.

But the Princess had stormed out of the room. Doxa reached behind him and picked up the flat, pointed end of his inky tail to prevent it causing any more problems and sadly followed behind, looking about as miserable and as solemn as anyone could in the Kingdom. Apart, of course, from the Keeper of the Royal Diary, who had had much more practice than the Carpet Dragon.

The rest of the morning was spent getting ready for the boat race. The boats were quite small and each had one brightly-coloured sail. There were two people in each boat. One moved the sail to make sure that the wind kept blowing the boat along. The other steered the boat with a wooden board that was tied on to the back of the boat. This steering board was held at one end while the other end was dipped into the water. Now both jobs were very important, but the Princess enjoyed steering the most. Anah always felt strangely pleased that simply by moving the steering board she could change the direction of the boat.

Now, while Anah got herself ready, the Emperor decided who should go in each boat.

The Carpenter needed someone small and light to help him, otherwise his boat would sink. So the Guardian of the Royal Treasures was asked. He was, of course, delighted to help in the green-sailed boat.

The Royal Tutors went together in the orange-sailed boat. The Royal Cook made an ideal match for the Collector of the Royal Books in the blue-sailed boat. But who could go with the Princess? Finally the Emperor made his choice.

He found the Keeper of the Royal Diary busy refilling his ink-pots, ready to record the afternoon's events.

"I'm glad I found you," said the Emperor, smiling widely. "I wondered if you were very busy this afternoon?"

"Oh well," sighed the Keeper of the Royal Diary very seriously, expecting the Emperor to ask him to record the results of the boat race. "Let me see in my diary. No, no. I don't think I'm doing anything else this afternoon so I would be delighted to help you, my Imperial Master."

"Oh good," smiled the Emperor. "In that case, I'm sure you won't mind going in the red-sailed boat this afternoon with my daughter."

"Oh!" came the surprised but solemn response.

". . . and," continued the Emperor, "her pet dragon." And with that he turned and left, leaving the open-mouthed, open-eyed, astonished and more than sombre-looking man with his open diary.

By that afternoon everything was made ready for the race. The boats, with their brightly-coloured sails, bobbed at their moorings on the thirty-second, thirty-third, thirty-fourth and thirty-fifth stepping stones. The Royal Tutors were arguing with each other and getting hopelessly tied up as they consulted endless scrolls about the correct way to sail the orange-sailed boat.

The Royal Cook was tying up the ropes of the blue sails in his boat like strings of sausages, while the Collector of the Royal Books had a quick snooze, leaning against the blue-sailed boat's steering board.

The huge figure of the Carpenter sat at the end of his green-sailed boat so as to steer it, but he was so heavy that the boat almost stuck upright out of the water, and the Guardian of the Royal Treasures spent most of his time climbing up the steeply-sloping deck and then sliding back down again.

In Anah's red-sailed boat things were not so cheerful. She had wanted to use the steering board, and, as usual, she got her way. But she was not very pleased that the Emperor insisted that her Carpet Dragon came with her, and so she decided to give Doxa some good advice.

"Now listen carefully," she began. "If your tail causes any trouble in this race, then you know what will happen?" And she reached for the Emperor's gift that she had again hung around her neck. "Anyway you just sit still. There's nothing for you to do. If you can't even look after your silly tail, then you certainly can't do something important like steering a boat!"

Doxa sat in the middle of the boat and held on tight to his flat, pointed tail and doubted if he would be a very good sailor.

The very sombre and serious Keeper of the Royal Diary concentrated hard and wished that he was somewhere else. If the truth were known, he did not much care for boats.

The four boats tugged at their moorings, the wind filling their brightly-coloured sails.

"Now are you ready?" called the Emperor. "When I say so, the race will begin. The first boat to sail completely around this city and come back to the stepping stones will win. On your marks . . . Go!" The Emperor lowered his hand smartly so that his golden woven cloak caught the sunlight and flashed a dazzling display.

Now the Royal Tutors in the orange-sailed boat were so tied up with long scrolls that they never actually saw the starting signal. So they were still arguing as the other three boats left their moorings.

Unfortunately, in the Royal Cook's blue-sailed boat, the Collector of the Royal Books had not woken up, which meant that instead of sailing around the island they sailed straight into it.

Meanwhile, the Guardian of the Royal Treasures did as well as he possibly could in the Carpenter's green-sailed boat, considering the circumstances.

In Anah's boat things went much better. They took an obvious early lead and were incredibly excited. Well, the Princess was incredibly excited. She called commands and advice to the Keeper of the Royal Diary, who tried his best to do as she told him, but was clearly not enjoying the experience at all.

Within a very short time it was clear that their boat was going to win. The wind kept the bright red sail billowed. Doxa held his tail in control and Anah steered magnificently. That was, until she decided to help the Keeper of the Royal Diary with the ropes. She let go of the steering board and leaned forward. The Keeper of the Royal Diary gasped in surprise and horror. The Princess looked back just in time to see the rope holding the steering board come unknotted, and the steering board itself slip overboard and float away.

The Princess cried out, "Who did that?" and the Keeper of the Royal Diary closed his eyes and solemnly reminded her that she had, and that they now had no way of steering their boat.

"Oh no!" cried Anah. "Now we shall lose!"

"Yes!" sighed the Keeper of the Royal Diary. "Yes, it looks as if we shall. I suppose we had better give up and just let the wind blow us safely to land." The Princess was sure that there was just the flicker of a smile on his solemn face as he suggested going back to dry land. But Anah wasn't beaten yet, and when she gazed behind and saw the strange-looking green-sailed boat of the Carpenter approaching slowly but surely, she was more determined than ever to finish the race.

"Oh, surely we can find another steering board. All we need is something that's long and flat," pleaded Anah. "But what can we use?" And then she suddenly remembered the small round stone that hung by a golden chain around her neck. Well, this was a real emergency. This was something that desperately needed changing, for they might have a serious accident if they couldn't steer properly. Surely the Emperor would expect her to use it now. Anyway there was nothing else she could do. Surely he wouldn't object to them winning the race. They were so close to the winning line and she could clearly see the sixty-six stepping stones. Oh . . . what could she do? Should she use the stone? There was nothing else to use. No one else had anything that could help. She looked at the Keeper of the Royal Diary, but he just shook his head. But as she reached for the stone that hung around her neck she noticed for the first time that afternoon that Doxa still sat holding his flat, pointed tail. She looked at the miserable Carpet Dragon and then suddenly she saw what she was looking for. It had been right in front of her!

"Oh! Ah, Doxa," she said slowly, putting the stone back. "My dear dragon, could we, er, possibly borrow your . . . your lovely tail for a moment?" Doxa was horrified. For one thing, he was so ashamed of his tail and its misbehaviour that he doubted anyone else could control it. And secondly, he doubted he could take it off to lend it to her, even if he wanted to.

"Doxa, we really do need it. It's very important." Doxa looked at the Princess with both red eyes. And as he did so she suddenly remembered all the unpleasant, unkind and hurtful things she had said about his tail. How up to a few moments ago she had wanted to be rid of it. How she had listened all day to what everyone had said about it. But now she saw it differently. She needed it more than anything else. She saw it as something important — as the only thing that could save her from having to use the stone. But she couldn't have just the tail! For the tail was part of Doxa! It was Doxa that was important. But after all she had said, she really wondered if he would help.

"Doxa, I'm sorry," she said, and suddenly it didn't sound foolish to talk to the dragon like that. So she went on. "It's not just your tail that is important right now — it's *you*. You alone can help us. Please will you use your tail. The Great Weaver has given it to you to use. Please, Doxa. You can really do it. I know you can save us and help us. If only you will use your tail."

Doxa was amazed. No one had ever said anything nice about his tail before. No one had ever wanted him to use it. No one had ever said that the Great Weaver had given it to him to use. He had always been ashamed of it but now his Princess wanted him to use it! He got up carefully and came and sat next to the Princess. The Keeper of the Royal Diary solemnly shook his head. He clearly did not approve and, for a moment, the Princess wondered if she was doing the right thing.

But then she remembered what the Emperor had said only the night before. "Yesterday," said Anah, quietly, but very determinedly, "you told me a story, and the Emperor said that even though we are all different, we are still all important, because the Great Weaver has made us. Doxa was made with a tail — and now he can use it for something really important. I'm glad Doxa's got a tail!"

"Now Doxa," she continued kindly. "Just dip your tail into the water behind the boat and face me. Your tail will do the rest." Doxa did as he was told. The water was very cold and, to be honest, it wasn't very comfortable even for a Carpet Dragon, but, sure enough, his tail behaved like a real steering board. It never misbehaved itself or did the wrong thing. For the first time he was very proud of the tail the Great Weaver had given him, and so was the Princess. The Keeper of the Royal Diary even looked for one moment as if he would smile.

In the Carpenter's boat they saw what had happened and that the race was now lost. But when the Guardian of the Royal Treasures cried out, "Oh drat that dragon's tail!" Doxa didn't mind at all and neither, really, did the Princess of the Kingdom of the Carpet Dragon.

8

The Candle-Light

Anah was pleased that she had not used the stone that day. Doxa was also feeling very pleased and very proud as he sat quietly at his Princess's feet. Everyone had again assembled in the great banqueting hall for a Royal Birthday celebration tea. Once more the oil lamps were lit and a still quietness settled on the banqueting room.

In the dim light the Collector of the Royal Books yawned and solemnly leaned towards Anah. He whispered, "Have you used it yet?"

"What?" she whispered back.

"The stone," he answered wearily.

"No, not yet," she replied.

"Oh, I just wondered . . ." he began, looking at the still and well-controlled, coiled tail of the Carpet Dragon. The Emperor, however, had noticed that the Collector of the Royal Books had woken up from his quiet doze, so he decided that this would be the best moment for the fourth of the Royal

Advisers' gifts.

"Anah, tonight the Collector of the Royal Books will tell you his story. It is his gift to you. It too will tell you more of the Great Weaver — but it will also tell you a great mystery. For you shall now learn where this golden cloak, which you will someday wear, came from."

Anah gasped and her eyes opened in anticipation. For she had often wondered where such a cloak could have been made.

"Ah? Ah, yes," sighed the Collector of the Royal Books, straightening his wispy white beard. "Princess! The Great Weaver has made many worlds and each of them has its own pattern and weaves its own story.

"There was once a very strange world. For half of the year the sun shone brightly overhead. It never truly became dark. But when the sun did set, it was gone for the other half of the year and throughout that winter it never truly became light. Those long winters were very cold, and the equally long summers were very warm. In that strange world of light or dark the most important of all jobs was that of the candle-maker. For during the long, light summer the candle-maker made candles, so that when the winter came and there was no more light

from the sun, everyone would be able to see.

"Now there came to that land one particularly great candle-maker. No one knew where he came from. But his candles burned brighter and longer than anyone else's. Everyone was amazed at the beauty of the candles and all who bought candles from him agreed that never had such marvellous objects been seen in the Kingdom. And so he soon became the Royal Candle-maker to the King himself.

"Now one hot summer this candle-maker made some candles whose wax was like liquid glass. They were so fine and beautiful that people came from all over the land to gaze into the candle-maker's shop window and admire his craftsmanship. This pleased the candle-maker. 'But', he said, 'They could be even finer if I had gold to decorate them with.'

" 'Then ask the King,' they said. 'He will give you gold if you only ask.' So the candle-maker asked the king, and the king gave him much gold to use in the making of these candles. The candle-maker made many candles with patterns of gold around their sides. These candles, in turn, made the candle-maker famous. But sadly, they also made him proud.

"The summer did not last for ever and,

as sometimes happens in that world after a particularly light and warm summer, the six months of winter darkness were especially cold. Indeed, so thickly did the snow fall that even in the grounds of the royal palace it soon piled up in huge drifts. After one particularly heavy storm it was discovered that the oil in the lamps that lit the palace was running low. But the snow had piled up thickly over the sheds in the courtyard where the oil was kept and before anyone could find the shovels to clear the snow, the oil in the lamps ran out. The palace was plunged into a deep darkness.

" 'Master,' said the King's most trusted servant. 'We have no light to find the shovels.'

" 'Then go to my Royal Candle-maker,' commanded the King. 'And tell him that we have need of candles to give us light to find the shovels.'

"The servant battled through the bitterly cold snow-covered streets and woke the candle-maker from a deep, winter's sleep.

" 'The King wants one of my fine candles for nothing better than to search for a shovel! Of all the nerve!' declared the candle-maker. 'He shall not have one of my candles for such a thing!' he shouted at the servant in the frozen street. And he slammed the door to his shop.

"The King's servant sadly turned back to the palace when a small wooden door opened at one of the nearby houses.

" 'Sir,' came the gentle voice of a poor woman. 'I could not help overhearing what was said. If the King has need of a light he may have our lamp.' She showed the servant the one, dimly-glowing lamp in the middle of a cold, cluttered room. Inside there huddled two small children.

"The King's servant smiled. 'You must bring it to the King yourself and your family must come as well.'

"When the King heard of what had happened, he welcomed the poor woman and her children and with the help of her lamp there was soon oil enough for all. The King insisted that for the rest of the winter she stayed at the palace to enjoy all the good things that were to be found there.

"That winter dragged on. Then one day there was a loud thump and a crash at one of the palace windows. The King went outside and found a beautiful bird lying exhausted in the snow. He gently picked up the cold, exhausted creature.

" 'We must give this poor creature some gentle warmth. For if we were to take it directly into the palace the shock would kill it. Go to the Candle-maker! Ask him to let us have one of his finest candles, so that we can use the gentle heat from it to warm this poor bird.'

"Again the King's servant battled through the icy streets to the Royal Candle-maker.

" 'The King wants what?' shouted the candle-maker. 'My candles are far too fine to waste on some wretched bird that should have flown to warmer lands weeks ago! The King shall not have one.' And with that the door was slammed again.

"The King's servant sadly turned to go, but as he passed the blacksmith's shop the door opened and out stepped the burly figure of the blacksmith.

" 'I could not help but hear what was said,' he began in his gruff voice. 'I still have some embers glowing in my forge. If the King needs warmth he shall have it.'

"The King's servant smiled. 'You shall bring the embers to him,' he said.

"The blacksmith shovelled up the glowing embers from his forge and put them on to a metal tray. He placed a lid over it and went with the King's servant to the palace where he placed the poor bird on to the gently warming lid of the tray. Soon the embers had warmed the frozen creature until its strength had returned and it would take food and could be taken safely into the palace.

" 'This bird and the blacksmith must stay in my palace until the night of winter is passed,' said the King when he heard of what had happened.

"The winter dragged on. There was little in that land to bring joy, but in the palace the King declared that they would have a mid-winter feast to cheer all the people in the land. Invitations were sent out. Everyone was to bring something to the feast. A huge cake was made.

" 'Go to my Royal Candle-maker,' demanded the King, 'and say we have need of candles to put on this cake to give us joy.' Again the King's servant set out. Again he knocked on the door of the candle-maker and explained that the King had need of some of his candles to decorate the cake to bring joy in the mid-winter celebrations. The candle-maker was furious.

" 'The King wants *my* candles to stick on a cake? How dare he insult me in this way! My candles are far too grand to be used for such a thing. The King shall not have them.' And again the door was slammed. The servant sadly turned to go. But, as he passed by a child playing in the snow, he felt a small hand slip something into his. He looked down at the child.

" 'I heard what you said about the King

wanting to decorate the cake. Here, take these,' said the child. The King's servant looked down into his hand and found some small brightly-coloured sweets. 'They're all I have, but the King can have them.'

" 'Then you shall give them to him. Come with me, you and your family, to the palace.' Again the King listened in sadness to his servant's story. He gladly received the child's gift and he and his family had places of honour at the mid-winter feast. But no one saw anything of the Royal Candle-maker.

"The winter dragged on. But one day the sun reappeared and although at first its light was weak and its warmth was little, each day it grew more brilliant and everyone knew that winter was over.

"Soon the snow had gone from the streets and people returned to their work. But the candle-maker had nothing to do! For his grand candles had not been used that winter. They still stood as beautiful as ever in the shop window.

"People still stopped and admired them. They looked at the beautiful patterns on the sides made of strands of pure gold. They looked at the clearness of the wax and the straightness of the wick and that pleased the candle-maker very much. But, as the sun grew hotter and its brightness shone on those candles all that summer, they slowly began to change. For the brightness of the sun faded the colour of the wax in the candles, and the warmth of the sun slowly melted them, so that they no longer stood tall and straight but sagged and wilted. No longer did anyone admire them, but rather they laughed at them, for they took on strange shapes as they leaned crazily into one another.

"When the candle-maker heard the people's laughter he was furious. He snatched the candles out of the shop window and looked at the faded, wilting, melting pools of wax and he knew they were of no use. The golden threads that he had used so carefully to decorate the candles were twisted and broken, and they pricked his fingers and hands as he snatched at the useless candles.

" 'Well!' sneered the candle-maker. 'If the king wants them he can have them now.' And he threw the pile of candles into an old cloth sack and took them to the palace. He threw them down at the palace doors and left them for the King. The candle-maker departed from that land that day and was never seen again.

"Now the sun shone brightly on that old sack until it became so warm that the wax melted and trickled its way through the sackcloth. But the gold strands were left behind. So when the King found the old sack and opened it, inside there were no faded wax candles at all, for all the wax had gone. Instead there were just strands of beautiful gold. And the King took them and it was a good thing that he did so, because some say that the King who ruled in that land was none other than the Great Weaver himself. And, it is said that those strands of gold were woven into a beautiful cloak, and that cloak always gave light and warmth and joy to all those who saw it.

"And, Princess, some even say that it is the very cloak that is now always worn by the ruler of this Kingdom."

"And, Anah," continued the Emperor, "whenever we look at this cloak we remember that all the good things that are given to us by the Great Weaver are given to be used and shared with others. That we cannot hold on to them jealously for ourselves, for in the end that will bring us no joy. But, Anah, sometimes it is very hard to give back that which we have been given."

But Anah was looking at the beauty of the golden cloak and could see herself reflected in the mirror-like shine and she couldn't help thinking, with a slight shudder, that one day it would be rightfully hers, for she was the Princess of the Kingdom of the Carpet Dragon.

9

The Happy-Return

The Princess of the Kingdom of the Carpet
Dragon watched as the morning sun streamed
in through the arch-shaped window in her
bedroom. Everything seemed so bright and
brilliant that the Princess felt as if the Great
Weaver had only just woven the land. Doxa
slept quietly and gently. His tail was neatly
coiled in front of his nose. His wings occasionally fluttered as if stretched in some dreamy
flight, and there were occasional puffs of
smoke drifting up from his nostrils.

The Princess was very proud of her Carpet
Dragon.

When Doxa eventually opened his red eyes
he was not at all surprised to find the Princess
already dressed.

'Doxa,' she said confidently. 'Today is the
last day of my Royal Birthday, so we shall
have to use the stone.'' He did not, for one
moment, doubt that she right.

All morning she searched in the city for
something important to change. With Doxa's

help she found many things that she didn't really have to use the stone to change — for she could do something about them for herself.

So when a loom broke while weaving a new and particularly fine carpet, it was Anah, who (with the help of the Royal Carpenter) cut the wood, and hammered the nails to secure it once more, and so changed the broken and useless muddle back into a smoothly clicking and clacking piece of machinery.

It was also Anah, with the help of Doxa, who prevented what could have been a terrible disaster. For while passing the Royal Kitchens she thought that she could smell something strange — something even stranger than normal. She looked in and saw that the kitchen was empty except for clouds of smoke coming from a saucepan. She saw that a wooden spoon had been left in the saucepan and the saucepan was still on the stove. Suddenly the wooden spoon burst into flames. She knew she wouldn't be able to do anything herself, for it was too dangerous — so she closed the kitchen door and ran with Doxa to find someone else. The first person she met was the Royal Cook — who soon had everything under control.

Everyone was pleased to see the Princess and her dragon. Unknown to her, she had been given a new name in the Kingdom, for they now called her the Carpet Dragon Princess. Not just because she was always to be seen with the Carpet Dragon, but more because, like a Carpet Dragon, she always seemed to be close at hand when there was trouble or need of any sort. Not that she was nosey, or interfered with things that didn't concern her. She was just . . . well . . . caring. In fact some people felt that since her Royal Birthday she actually seemed to be looking for things to do and people to help. Some even said she was more like a servant than a Princess. But she was still herself. She still wore the same practical clothes. She was still as lively and unpredictable, even at breakfast time.

She had been a little surprised that her father, the Emperor, did not join them for breakfast. But her mother told her that the Emperor had left very early that morning to visit the lands around the city.

Anah spent the last day of her Royal Birthday happily with her Carpet Dragon, looking for something that was worthy of being changed by her stone. But in her heart she began to doubt that she would ever use it.

However, just before sunset, Anah, the Princess of the Kingdom of the Carpet Dragon, eventually discovered that she would have to use the stone.

She had crossed the sixty-six stones to run and walk in the forest land that surrounded the lake. She wasn't any longer looking for anything special to change. In fact she had accepted the fact that she would not use the stone. She turned to look at the Emperor's island in the middle of the lake and saw Doxa flying high above the Royal Palace. Puffs of smoke were being left by him in a trail across the sky, and his tail swished and flicked behind him. Anah felt very proud of Doxa. She sighed happily and decided to go back to the Palace. She walked across the sixty-six stepping stones and up the ramp.

Suddenly, as she was about to enter through the city gates, she heard a voice from behind her. She thought she recognized it at once, and turned, but there in the dim light of the evening stood before her the poorest and most wretched person she had ever seen.

There was nothing frightening about him. And she knew she was quite safe in the Emperor's city, for nothing harmful ever crossed the stones. But she had never seen anyone in so much need. He had no shoes. No curly-toed carpet slippers. His hair was untidy and his dark eyes were full of sadness. His hands were rough from hard work and he was wrapped in the poorest and most ragged cloak she had ever seen.

She had never met anyone in the Kingdom who looked so poor.

Without a moment's thought she reached into her pocket to find something to give to him, but she found nothing. Surely there was something she could give. She felt about her — and then discovered the one thing she had to give. The Emperor's gift. Her greatest gift. The Princess unfastened the golden clip and held the golden chain and the stone in her hand.

Suddenly she realized how precious it was to her, even though she had decided that it would never now be used for the purpose it was given. For it was her present. And, after all, who was this stranger? Perhaps he didn't belong to the Kingdom. Surely someone else could do something. But deep inside she knew that she was the only one who could help. And suddenly she found how hard it was to give. Yet as she looked at the golden chain she remembered the Emperor's golden cloak — and how the Emperor had given the stone to her, not to someone else. She had been given it to use! Oh . . . it was very confusing. If she gave the chain and stone away, how would it change anything?

Surely this wasn't how the Emperor's gift was to be used? She had always imagined that when the time came to use the stone she would rub it, or speak to it, or that something strange and wonderful would happen. But now, as she stood there, she knew that she was simply going to have to give it away. For she knew the golden chain and the stone would seem like a fortune to someone so poor.

It took all her strength to reach out and say, "Please. It's all I have. You have it." Yet she gave her Royal Birthday present to the poorest person in the Kingdom of the Carpet Dragon. Although she felt bewildered she didn't feel sad — in fact, she felt strangely happy. She turned to run back into the city to tell the Emperor what had happened, when suddenly the ragged figure spoke again.

"My Royal Princess," he cried in joy and triumph.

She turned and there was the poor man as she had last seen him, but as he pushed the ragged and torn rags aside she saw the golden robe of the Emperor himself and, as his eyes filled with joy, she realized that it was her father. She had given the Emperor's gift back to her father; she had returned his own gift.

"But, Father!" cried the astonished Princess. "What are you doing dressed like that?"

"I was doing what the Great Weaver required," he said simply.

Anah looked down at the stone the Emperor held in his hand. A strange feeling of disappointment rose in her as she looked at the stone.

"But, Father," sighed Anah. "I never did find something to change! I never used the stone."

"Not so, Anah," the Emperor gently replied, taking Anah by the hand. "You did use it! And it did change the one thing that it could change."

Anah looked totally confused. And it was at that moment that Doxa, the Carpet Dragon, decided to practise his landing. Unfortunately it was not one of his best. He slid and skidded and eventually came to a halt as he collided with Anah, the Princess of the Kingdom of the Carpet Dragon.

10

The Greatest-Gift

Anah was, to say the least, a little surprised at having a Carpet Dragon land on her. Doxa sighed deeply and a cloud of smoke surrounded them.

"Do you know, Doxa," sighed Anah, "there are times when I wish you hadn't changed into . . ." But then she suddenly stopped. "That's it," she cried. "That's it . . . the stone . . . it did work . . . it changed Doxa!"

"No, Princess," said the Emperor, "*it* did not change the dragon. For Anah, you helped change Doxa."

"I did?" gasped Anah.

"Yes . . ." affirmed the Emperor. "You did. But you only did it because, Princess, the stone changed *you*!"

"Me!" gasped Anah.

"Yes, Anah, you!" For a moment Anah was very worried. She quickly looked down at herself. She certainly didn't look different; nor did she feel different.

"Anah, the stone has no magic, no mystery.

It simply made you look, and think and care. It helped you to learn about the Great Weaver and to put what you learned into practice. It has turned you into a Real Princess. For anyone who rules in this Kingdom must learn to serve it. To help and care for the needs of all who live in it . . . even a dragon. Anah, this stone could only change one thing in this Kingdom . . . and that was you!''

Anah looked in total astonishment.

That night, as they all again sat in the banqueting hall and the lamps had again been lit, the Emperor leaned towards Anah and said in a loud voice,

"Well, Anah . . . did you use it?''

"What, Father?'' she answered.

"The stone,'' he replied.

"Yes, Father. I did.''

"It is true,'' said the Emperor triumphantly. "The stone has done its job well, as have the Royal Advisers. Anah is now a Real Princess. For she has learned how caring for others can change things in this Kingdom.''

Anah was very pleased. Now she knew that to be a Real Princess she didn't have to wear a golden tiara, or learn how to curtsey, but rather to remember all that she had learned about the Great Weaver and the Kingdom of the Carpet Dragon on her Royal Birthday.

"And now, Anah," continued the Emperor. "Because the Great Weaver has helped you to use your first Royal Birthday gift wisely, we would like you to have a new gift."

The Emperor gave the Princess a large and beautifully wrapped package. Doxa opened a red eye to see what was going on.

"Ah," thought the Keeper of the Royal Diary. "Perhaps at last it's a silken bonnet." But it wasn't.

"Ah," thought the Collector of the Royal Books. "Perhaps at last it's a *Complete History of the Kingdom in Twelve Volumes.*" But it wasn't.

"Ah," thought the Guardian of the Royal Treasures. "Perhaps at last it's a golden tiara." But it wasn't.

Instead it was a small, rough stone on a golden chain, wrapped up in a beautifully woven golden robe. And embroidered on that robe was a picture of a flying, purple Carpet Dragon, wearing red, curly-toed carpet slippers, breathing smoke and waving a proud tail.

"Princess," whispered the Emperor. "Wear this for me."

And she always did. For although the years passed and Anah never did learn how to curtsey, and was never very fond of golden tiaras and dusty books, and found it impossible to remember all those important dates and names from the past, she never forgot that Royal Birthday and the things that she learned from the Great Weaver.

So, many years later, after Anah and Doxa, with the help of the Great Weaver, had been on other great adventures, it was decided to set all of these things down. But not in a dull and dusty book. No. Instead, a wonderful carpet was woven – that told the story of Anah, and Doxa, and the Great Weaver's Kingdom.

And, who knows? Because that carpet was woven where the sun rises, and its colours can never completely fade, if you were now to find that carpet you might just see the Kingdom of the Carpet Dragon come once more to life . . .

Also from Lion Publishing

UNDER THE GOLDEN THRONE

Ralph Batten

"Under the golden throne, in the palace of the High King, lay Shamar, the one and only dog of Patria. Slowly he yawned and opened a big, brown eye . . ."

In the seven tales of Shamar the dog, we meet a wealth of comic characters including the self-important Prime Minister of Patria, the fussy Chancellor of the Exchequer and the dignified Derel the Wise. And, of course, the delightfully stupid Seven Knights of the Realm.

Each story tells of an adventure of Shamar the dog and his beloved master, the High King of Patria. And at the end of each story, Shamar settles down under the golden throne and sleeps. And as he sleeps, he dreams a dream . . .

The Haffertee Stories

Janet and John Perkins

Haffertee is a soft-toy hamster. Ma Diamond made him for her little girl, Yolanda (usually known as Diamond Yo), when her real pet hamster died.

These books tell the adventures of the inquisitive, amusing and lovable Haffertee Hamster – at home, at school and in the world outside.

There are six Haffertee books in the series. Illustrated with line drawings, each contains ten short stories, ideal for bedtime reading or reading aloud.

HAFFERTEE HAMSTER
HAFFERTEE'S NEW HOUSE
HAFFERTEE GOES EXPLORING
HAFFERTEE'S FIRST CHRISTMAS
HAFFERTEE GOES TO SCHOOL
HAFFERTEE'S FIRST EASTER